A SOLDIER'S JOURNEY

Laura Shenton

A SOLDIER'S JOURNEY

Laura Shenton

Iridescent Toad Publishing

Iridescent Toad Publishing.

First edition. ISBN 978-1-913779-22-1

Chapter One

The town square bustled with the unbridled energy of a community caught between the comfortable rhythms of daily life and the gathering storm clouds of impending war. It was the height of summer in 1914. Market stalls lined the cobbled streets in neat rows, their wooden frames creaking beneath displays of fresh produce and household goods. Vendors called out their prices in singsong voices that echoed off the stone buildings, while harried mothers corralled their unruly children with firm hands and stern words. Men gathered in tight clusters, their conversations hushed and wary, their expressions bearing the shadow of news from distant capitals.

Among the swirling crowd stood Charlie Greenly, a fifteen-year-old boy whose lanky frame had just begun to fill out with the promise of manhood. His head swam with intoxicating stories of glory and valour. For weeks now, he had been listening intently to the rumours that swept through the town – urgent talk of war, of the pressing need for brave men to step forward and defend their country against foreign aggression. The newspapers had begun printing increasingly alarming headlines of alliances and hostilities, of ultimatums and mobilisations, and now, at last, the recruiters had arrived in town, their presence transforming the familiar square.

Charlie stood shoulder-to-shoulder with his best friend, James Cooper, both boys stretching their necks to peer over the heads of the gathering crowd. Their eyes were fixed on the hastily constructed wooden platform where a uniformed officer, his brass buttons gleaming in the summer sun, addressed the growing throng with the authority of a man who knew the weight of his words. The officer's voice carried across the square, powerful and commanding, cutting through the persistent hum of market-day conversation.

"The time has come, men of England!" he

proclaimed, his chest swelling beneath his crisp uniform. "Your country calls upon you in her hour of need! We must stand united in defence of King and country! Let not the German Kaiser and his armies think Britain weak or unwilling! This is your moment – your chance to be part of history itself. Fight for honour, for your families, for the very future of our great British Empire!"

A murmur swept through the onlookers, growing stronger with each passing moment. Some men exchanged meaningful glances, their faces etched with the internal struggle between their responsibilities at home and the inexorable pull of patriotic duty. Others nodded with grim determination, their decisions already firm, ready to step forward and sign their names in the leather-bound recruitment ledger.

Charlie felt his pulse quicken beneath his collar, each beat a drummer's call to action. This, he knew with the fierce certainty of youth, was his moment – his chance to break free from the confines of small-town life and prove himself worthy of the stories he'd read about brave soldiers and noble sacrifices. In his mind's eye, he could already see himself in a smart uniform, rifle in hand, marching proudly through the streets of France.

James turned to him then, his face flushed with excitement, his eyes bright with possibility. "We should do it, Charlie," he said, his voice trembling with barely contained enthusiasm. "We should sign up together."

Charlie hesitated for only the briefest moment, his conscience wrestling with the knowledge that he wasn't old enough – not officially. However, he had broad shoulders for his age, and his voice had already deepened into something that could pass for a man's. He knew of others – boys not much older than himself – who had successfully enlisted by telling a simple lie about their age. If he carried himself properly and spoke with confidence, no one would think to question him too closely.

Drawing himself up to his full height, Charlie squared his shoulders with determination. "Let's go," he said.

The two boys pushed their way through the press of bodies, threading between concerned mothers and excited young men until they reached the recruiters' station, where a long wooden table had been set up. Behind it sat a sergeant with a carefully waxed moustache, his eyes sharp beneath the brim of his cap as he surveyed each potential recruit. He looked up as Charlie and James approached, his gaze measuring them with the practiced eye of a man who had seen hundreds of eager young faces in recent days.

"How old are you, lad?" the sergeant asked Charlie directly, his eyes narrowing slightly as he took in Charlie's youthful features.

"Eighteen, sir," Charlie replied without hesitation, willing his voice to remain steady and clear. He met the sergeant's gaze, trying to project a confidence he didn't entirely feel.

The sergeant studied him for what felt like an eternity, his expression unreadable. Charlie held his breath, his heart hammering so loudly in his chest that he was certain everyone in the square could hear it.

Then, with the ghost of a knowing smirk playing at the corners of his mouth, the sergeant gave a slight nod. "Good man," he said, passing the clipboard across the rough wooden surface of the table.

Charlie's hand trembled slightly as he took it, gripping the pen with more force than necessary. He signed his name in careful letters, willing them to appear as steady and mature as possible. Each stroke of the pen felt momentous, permanent, like carving his future into stone.

Charlie's signature was barely dry on the paper when the sergeant barked, "Next!" with the mechanical efficiency of a man who had processed countless recruits before. A steady stream of men followed in Charlie's wake. Some were young and eager like himself and James, their eyes bright with dreams of glory. Others were older and more weathered, their faces etched with the quiet resolve of men who understood duty's price more deeply than the younger ones.

Charlie stepped aside from the recruitment table, his heart racing with an intoxicating exhilaration that made his head swim. The town square had transformed into a crucible of excitement, the air thick with the fevered conversations of new recruits speaking in eager tones about their upcoming adventure. Across the street, a kaleidoscope of recruitment posters fluttered against the weathered walls of the post office and the Crown & Anchor pub – bold, colourful images of determined soldiers with bayonets raised high, marching in perfect formation beneath gloriously unfurled Union Jacks. The artists had captured exactly what Charlie felt in his heart: the romance of war, the nobility of sacrifice, the certainty of victory.

James nudged Charlie's ribs with his elbow, his face transformed by a beam of pure joy. "We did it!" he exclaimed, his voice cracking with emotion. "We actually did it!"

Charlie nodded, still somewhat breathless from the magnitude of what they'd just done. "We did," he agreed, the words feeling strange and wonderful on his tongue.

They had all grown up on stirring tales of England's military might – stories of Waterloo, where Wellington's forces had crushed Napoleon's dreams of empire; of Agincourt, where English longbowmen had decimated the flower of French chivalry; of countless other victories that had built and maintained British supremacy across the globe. The newspapers spoke with absolute certainty that this war would be no different – a quick, decisive conflict that would see the Germans thoroughly defeated before they could pose any real threat to the British way of life. Even the recruiter, with his brass buttons and air of authority, had assured them that the Kaiser's army would crumble before the might of the British Empire.

In his mind's eye, Charlie could already see himself marching triumphantly through these very streets, resplendent in a sharp uniform with gleaming medals adorning his chest. Perhaps the King himself would recognise their bravery, their sacrifice for the Empire. The fantasy felt so real he could almost taste it.

Near the enlistment table, a group of well-dressed young women moved through the crowd with purpose, armed with delicate white feathers. They pressed these symbols of cowardice into the hands of young men who had not yet signed their names to the recruitment rolls, their pretty faces twisted with contempt for those who hesitated. "Cowards," someone in the crowd muttered as a red-faced young man turned away, the white feather trembling between his fingers like an accusation.

Charlie and James shared a look of smug certainty – they would never know such shame. They had proven themselves men today, not boys who needed to be shamed into doing their duty.

It was then that Charlie caught sight of his father standing at the edge of the square, half-hidden in the shadow of the cobbler's shop. Mr Greenly's expression was impossible to read, hovering somewhere between pride and something darker, more complex – something that made Charlie's stomach tighten unexpectedly.

Drawing himself up to his full height, Charlie walked over to his father with measured steps, trying to project the confidence of a soldier rather than a boy seeking approval. "I signed up," he announced, the words coming out more quietly than he'd intended.

There was a long pause, heavy with unspoken thoughts.

Then, finally, his father gave a slow, deliberate nod. "You're a man now," he said, the words falling between them with an uncomfortable finality.

It was not the reaction Charlie had expected or hoped for. His father's gaze was steady but somehow distant, as though he was looking through Charlie rather than at him – as though he was seeing not the soldier-to-be who stood before him, but rather the small boy who had once needed help climbing the apple tree in their garden.

Before Charlie could find the right words to respond, his father extended his hand – rough and calloused from years of honest work – into the space between them. Charlie hesitated for just a heartbeat before taking it. His father's grip was firm, encompassing, somehow both familiar and strange.

"Do your duty," he said, each word weighted with meaning Charlie couldn't quite grasp.

Charlie swallowed hard against a sudden tightness in his throat. As he watched his father retreat into the crowd, a tiny flicker of uncertainty took root.

Chapter Two

The week that followed passed in a whirlwind of preparation and anticipation, each day both dragging endlessly and rushing by with frightening speed. Life had taken on a dreamlike quality, as if everything Charlie had known was slowly dissolving into something new and strange.

Everywhere he went, the town hummed with an electric current of excitement. The newspaper sellers called out headlines of British mobilisation with unprecedented vigour, their voices carrying tales of German weakness and inevitable Allied victory through the narrow streets. Each day brought fresh assurances that the Kaiser's army was ill-prepared, that German morale was low, that victory was not just certain but imminent. The local shops had transformed into informal gathering places where people shared the latest news and rumours with breathless enthusiasm. The bakers and butchers who had known Charlie since he was toddling after his mother now greeted him with respectful nods, treating him not as the boy who once stole apples from Mr Harrison's cart, but as a man in uniform – or at least, soon to be.

At home, Charlie threw himself into his usual chores with renewed enthusiasm, keen to show he could still be depended upon even as he prepared to leave. He carried water from the well in heavy buckets, the wooden yoke pressing into his shoulders with familiar weight. He chopped firewood until his arms ached, each swing of the axe feeling like practice for some undefined future challenge. All the while, he tried to ignore the way his mother watched him when she thought he wasn't looking – her eyes following his movements with a desperate intensity, as if trying to memorise every detail of her son before he changed into something else entirely.

His younger sisters, Elisabeth and Mary, had developed a habit of whispering behind doors and around corners, stealing glances at him as though he had already transformed into one of the heroic figures from their beloved storybooks. Elisabeth, at twelve, was old enough to understand something of what was happening, and her usual teasing had given way to a sort of reverent silence. Even six-year-old Mary, who normally couldn't keep a secret to save her life, had grown unusually quiet in his presence.

On the final evening before he was set to leave for training, his mother outdid herself preparing a feast that would have been worthy of Christmas Day. The kitchen had been a flurry of activity since dawn, and now the table groaned under the weight of a magnificent spread – a perfectly roasted joint of beef that must have cost a week's wages, thick slices of fresh bread still warm from the oven, golden-brown potatoes swimming in gravy, and even a treacle tart for afters. It was a celebration fit for a returning hero, though Charlie hadn't yet left to earn such honours.

The family gathered around the table in the warm glow of candlelight, the familiar scene taking on an almost sacred quality. Charlie ate heartily, trying to soak in every detail of the moment – the way the candlelight flickered across the worn tablecloth, the sound of his sisters' feet scuffling under the table, the familiar creak of his father's chair. Soon, he told himself, he would return victorious, and they would all be proud of him. Soon, this ordinary scene would be transformed by his achievements into something legendary.

Across the table, his father set down his fork with deliberate care and fixed Charlie with a penetrating look that seemed to cut through all pretence. "You remember everything I taught you?"

The question carried the weight of years of father-son conversations, of lessons learned in the garden and the workshop, of wisdom passed down through generations of Greenly men.

Charlie straightened instinctively under that steady gaze. "Yes, sir," he replied, his voice firm despite the sudden tightness in his throat.

"Discipline, respect, courage," his father said, each word measured and precise. "The army will make you a man, but don't lose yourself in it. Remember who you are beneath the uniform."

Charlie's shoulders squared of their own accord. "I won't, I promise."

His father's eyes lingered on him for a long moment, searching for something in his son's face. Then, slowly, he nodded, pushing his barely-touched plate aside and rising from the table with the heavy movement of a man carrying an invisible burden.

Charlie watched him go, that familiar sliver of doubt creeping back into his mind.

Later that night, as Charlie methodically packed his few belongings into a small canvas bag, the sound of soft footsteps in the hallway announced his mother's approach. She appeared in the doorway of his bedroom like a ghost, her hands clasped tightly in front of her worn apron, her knuckles white with tension. The lamplight caught the silver threads in her hair – *When had those appeared?* Charlie wondered with a sudden pang of guilt.

"I'll keep your room just as you leave it, Charlie," she said softly, her voice carrying an undercurrent of emotion that made him pause in his careful folding of socks and undergarments.

Something in her tone had frozen his hands in place. The words themselves spoke of his return, but her voice – that gentle, familiar voice that had soothed countless childhood fears – trembled with an unspoken terror that he might never come back at all.

Charlie forced a smile, trying to inject certainty into his voice. "I'll be back before you know it, Mum. You'll hardly have time to miss me."

His mother smiled in return, but it was a brittle thing that didn't reach her eyes. Those eyes, which had watched over him for fifteen years, now seemed to be memorising his face, storing away every detail. "I know, love," she said, but the words sounded hollow, as though she was speaking them only because they were expected.

She crossed the room with quiet steps and pressed a kiss to his forehead, just as she had done every night when he was small. Her lips felt cool against his skin, and he caught the familiar scent of bread and lavender soap that had always meant home and safety and love.

When she left, closing the door with exquisite gentleness behind her, Charlie sat heavily on the edge of his narrow bed, staring at the half-packed bag as if it held answers to questions he hadn't even thought to ask.

The war was supposed to be glorious. Over by Christmas. An adventure to tell his children about someday.

So why did his mother look like she was already grieving?

Chapter Three

Morning arrived with cruel swiftness, pale sunlight creeping through Charlie's window like an unwelcome reminder of what was to come. He had barely slept, his mind too full of competing images – glorious victories and his mother's eyes, proud marches and his father's stern face, adventure and loss all tangled together in an impossible knot.

He stood now by the front door, his bag slung over his shoulder, feeling simultaneously larger and smaller than he ever had before. His uniform wouldn't come until later, but already he felt transformed – as if the mere act of enlisting had begun to reshape him into something more than a boy, though not quite yet a man.

His mother fussed over his coat with trembling hands, buttoning it up to his chin despite the warm summer air that already promised another sweltering day. "You've packed enough socks?" she asked for what must have been the tenth time that morning, smoothing down the fabric over his shoulders as if she could iron out the uncertainty in her heart through this simple, maternal gesture.

Charlie managed a small smile, trying to keep his voice light. "Yes, Mum. Enough socks for the whole army."

She pressed her lips together in a tight line and nodded, but her hands didn't leave his shoulders, as if letting go would somehow make his departure real and irreversible.

His father stood further back in the narrow hallway, arms crossed over his chest, watching the scene unfold with an unreadable expression. He had already said what needed to be said the night before – anything more would have been unnecessary, even inappropriate, for a Greenly man.

Elisabeth and Mary stood huddled together on the lower steps of the staircase in their nightdresses, their hair still mussed from sleep. They looked impossibly young and vulnerable in the early morning light.

Charlie forced a grin in their direction, desperate to lift the heavy atmosphere that had settled over the house. "Now, you two had better behave while I'm gone," he said with strained cheerfulness. "No stealing biscuits when Mum's not looking, and no using my room for your dolls' tea parties."

Mary giggled reflexively at his teasing tone, but Elisabeth – sweet, perceptive Elisabeth – frowned, her face pinched with worry beyond her years. "You will come back, won't you, Charlie?" she asked, voicing the fear that hung unspoken in every corner of the house.

Charlie ruffled her hair, just as he had done countless times before, trying to make the gesture feel normal, ordinary, unchanged. "Of course I will," he said with all the conviction he could muster. "Can't let you two run wild forever, can I?"

He said it with confidence, because it had to be true, didn't it? The war wouldn't last long – everyone said so. It would be quick and glorious. He would send letters home filled with tales of France, of victory marches through liberated towns, of medals pinned to his chest by grateful generals. He would make them all proud.

His mother finally stepped away, blinking rapidly against tears she refused to let fall. Charlie straightened his posture, adjusting the strap of his bag on his shoulder, feeling the weight of more than just his few possessions.

Then, at last, his father stepped forward, his presence filling the narrow hallway.

"You're a Greenly," he said, his voice carrying the legacy of generations. "Greenlys aren't quitters. We see things through to the end, whatever comes."

Charlie nodded, straightening his back instinctively. "No, sir. We don't quit."

His father's gaze held him for a long moment, searching his face as if trying to reconcile the child he had raised with the soldier-to-be who stood before him. Then he gave a single, firm nod – a gesture that contained all the pride, fear, and love that would never be spoken aloud.

And just like that, it was time.

Charlie opened the door, stepping out into the fresh morning air that smelt of dew and possibility.

As he walked further from his childhood home, the world looked exactly as it always had – the familiar cobbled streets winding their way through the town, the neat row of cottages with their well-tended gardens, the comforting scent of bread drifting from the bakery in the square. Yet everything felt different, as if he were seeing it all through new eyes, or perhaps for the last time.

The train station had transformed overnight into a festival ground of patriotic fervour. The usually quiet platform now hummed with an energy that seemed to vibrate through the wooden planks. Everywhere Charlie looked, he saw a sea of faces – fresh-faced recruits still in their civilian clothes, families clutching handkerchiefs, young boys watching with undisguised envy as their older brothers and friends prepared to depart for glory.

Charlie stood among them, his bag hanging heavy from his shoulder, watching the Union Jacks flutter proudly from every lamp post and awning. The local brass band had assembled near the ticket booths, their instruments gleaming in the sun as they played a stirring rendition of *Rule, Britannia!* The music soared over the platform, filling every young man's heart with an intoxicating mixture of pride, destiny, and unshakeable certainty in the righteousness of their cause.

James Cooper emerged from the crowd and clapped Charlie on the back, his familiar face flushed with excitement. "This is it, Charlie," he said, grinning ear to ear. "First step to glory, just like we talked about."

Charlie returned the smile, pushing down the last lingering doubts that tried to surface. "Over by Christmas, I hope?"

"Too right," James said with unshakeable confidence. "We'll be back before the first frost, covered in medals."

A few feet away, Arthur "Artie" Reynolds – another of the new recruits they'd met at the recruitment office – let out a booming laugh that drew several heads. He was a stocky lad with perpetually tousled hair and a mischievous glint in his eye, outspoken but the sort who would be welcomed as an ally in any scrape.

"Back by Christmas?" he scoffed, loud enough for nearby families to hear. "I say let's have our fun while we're out there! Good French wine, good French girls..."

A passing sergeant overheard and shot him a withering glare. "Less talk, more standing straight. You're a soldier now, not a music hall comedian."

Artie responded with an exaggerated pose of perfect military bearing that drew chuckles from the other recruits, though Charlie noticed he kept a wary eye on the sergeant's retreating back.

Charlie found himself laughing despite the knot in his stomach, grateful for this moment of lightness. It felt good to be among lads his own age, all sharing in the same grand adventure. Here, among his peers, there was no room for fear or doubt – only camaraderie and the intoxicating promise of glory to come.

As it approached, the train's whistle pierced the air, its sound like a clarion call. Steam billowed up against the blue sky, and the excitement on the platform swelled to fever pitch as the crowd erupted into cheers and shouts of encouragement.

"Make us proud, boys!" someone called out.

"Give the Hun what for!"

"Show them what British lads are made of!"

For the briefest moment, Charlie felt something twist inside him – a sudden, sharp awareness of all he was leaving behind.

Then the train pulled in with a great hiss of steam and screech of brakes, impossible to ignore. Doors opened along its length, and soldiers – real soldiers, already in their crisp uniforms – stepped out, barking orders for the recruits to board.

James grabbed Charlie's shoulder with trembling excitement. "Come on, then!"

Charlie gripped his bag tighter, feeling the rough canvas beneath his fingers, the last tangible connection to his civilian life. Then he stepped onto the train, the metal step ringing hollow beneath his foot.

The doors shut behind him with a finality that made his heart skip. The whistle blew, loud and clear. The engine shuddered and roared.

And just like that, Charlie Greenly was on his way to war.

Chapter Four

The train rumbled beneath Charlie's boots with a persistent, rhythmic clanking. The iron wheels ground against the tracks, their mechanical song filling the charged silence that now hung between conversations. In the early hours of the journey, the carriages had been alive with animated chatter – eager voices trading grandiose fantasies of war, spinning tales of heroism, and dreaming aloud of returning home to a hero's welcome. But as the hours had worn on and the familiar landscape blurred past the windows, the excited talk had gradually dwindled to whispers, then to nothing at all.

Charlie sat pressed against the window, his forehead occasionally brushing the cool glass as he watched the English countryside roll past. The patchwork of fields stretched out before him like a well-worn quilt – green squares of pasture, golden rectangles of wheat, and the dark browns of freshly ploughed soil. Soon enough, these comforting sights would give way to foreign lands he'd only read about in newspapers or seen in grainy photographs. The thought felt disorientating.

James, seated close enough that their shoulders touched, couldn't seem to keep still. He'd been fidgeting with his cap for the better part of an hour, turning it over and over in his hands until the wool was nearly worn smooth.

"Reckon we'll get our uniforms straight away?" he asked, his voice carrying a hint of nervous energy that seemed to speak for them all.

Artie, lounging on the opposite bench with an affected casualness that fooled no one, flashed his trademark grin. "Hope so. Can't wait to see how dashing I'll look in it." His words carried a forced lightness that didn't quite mask the uncertainty beneath.

The men around them chuckled, the sound tinged with relief at this small break in the tension. Even Charlie managed a smirk, though he felt the weight of his decision settle deeper in his chest, like a stone sinking through still water. In some ways, it felt as though they were all playing at being men.

As the conductor moved through the carriage with practiced efficiency, the recruits instinctively straightened, as if already responding to military discipline. Each young man leaned forward slightly, eager to catch any morsel of information about what awaited them.

"All new men are to report for training immediately upon arrival," the conductor announced, his voice carrying the weight of someone who'd seen countless groups of young men make this same journey. "You'll be under the command of Sergeant Davies – a fine man, but I wouldn't cross him." He added this last bit with a knowing look that made Charlie's stomach tighten.

Charlie exchanged a meaningful glance with James, both of them recognising that the sergeant already sounded far more serious than the cheerful recruiting officer who'd signed their papers with such enthusiasm.

***

The train's whistle pierced the air with a sharp blast, signalling their final approach.

James exhaled deeply beside Charlie, rolling his shoulders as if preparing to carry a great weight. "This is it, then." The words carried all the finality of a church bell's toll.

Charlie could only nod, his throat too tight for words.

The train slowed with a series of shudders, steam hissing from its flanks. Then, with a final, bone-jarring lurch, it ground to a halt with a screech of its brakes.

The doors slammed open, sudden and loud, making several recruits jump.

Outside, row upon row of soldiers stood waiting, their uniforms pressed to knife-edge perfection, their boots gleaming like black mirrors in the afternoon sun. They stood with ramrod-straight backs, faces set in masks of professional indifference. These weren't the fresh-faced boys from the recruitment posters – these were real soldiers, hardened by training and discipline.

Charlie had never seen anything like it. He

swallowed hard, his Adam's apple bobbing against the confining collar of his civilian shirt. He could feel sweat beginning to bead along his hairline.

"Out! Move, move, move!"

The moment Charlie's boots hit the platform, more shouting came from every direction, a bombardment of orders that seemed designed to disorientate and overwhelm. Sergeants materialised from nowhere, their voices cutting through the confusion, herding the recruits into roughly ordered lines with the efficiency of sheepdogs working a flock, the sound of their boots thunderous against the wooden planking.

Charlie found himself shoulder to shoulder with James and Artie, his knuckles white around the handle of his bag. Ahead of them stood a man who seemed to embody every story Charlie had ever heard about military discipline. He was tall and broad-shouldered, with a thick moustache that seemed carved from bronze and eyes that could have pierced armour plate. His uniform fit him like a second skin, every crease exactly where it should be, every button gleaming like a star.

Charlie recognised the type immediately – the kind of man who could smell weakness like a hunting dog scents prey. No-nonsense, hard as iron.

The man paced the line of recruits with deliberate slowness, his boots striking the platform with measured precision. His gaze swept over each face, seeming to catalogue every flaw, every hint of uncertainty.

"Some of you," the man began, his voice as gravelly as the railway ballast and just as unforgiving, "think this is a game." He paused, letting the words hang in the air. "I'm Sergeant Davies," he added, "and you're about to learn what it means to be a soldier."

Not a single recruit dared to move. Even breathing seemed dangerous.

"I see the smiles," the sergeant continued, his eyes narrowing. "The bravado." He stopped abruptly in front of a particularly young-looking recruit. "What's your name, boy?"

"Thompson, sir," the recruit stammered, his voice cracking on the second syllable.

Sergeant Davies studied him with intensity. "How old are you, Thompson?"

The silence that followed seemed to stretch for an eternity.

"Eighteen, sir," Thompson finally managed, the lie as transparent as glass.

Sergeant Davies released a snort that contained volumes of disbelief. "Eighteen, is it?" His gaze swept across the assembled recruits. "Let me tell you something, lads. The enemy doesn't care how old you are. They don't give a damn."

A cold silence fell over the recruits, broken only by the distant sound of a train whistle and the flutter of a Union Jack in the breeze. The sergeant let the silence hit home, watching as the reality of the situation began to sink in.

"You are no longer boys," he said firmly. "You are soldiers. And I will make damn sure you act like it."

Chapter Five

Charlie barely had time to register the growing ache in his shoulders from his hastily discarded bag before the urgency of military preparation swept him forward. The world became a blur of movement and barked orders, each moment carrying him further from civilian life.

The uniform issue took place in a long, low-ceilinged building that smelt of mothballs and new wool. Steam pipes clanked overhead, and the air was thick with the peculiar mixture of textile dust and sweat. The garments were made of stiff, unyielding wool in a shade of khaki that seemed to strip away individuality as effectively as it did colour. The fabric scratched against Charlie's skin like sandpaper, a sensation he suspected he'd never quite get used to. His boots, when they came, were two sizes too large, the leather uncomfortably rigid.

"You'll grow into them," the quartermaster barked, his voice carrying the weariness of a man who'd equipped hundreds, perhaps thousands, of recruits before him.

Charlie watched as James tried to negotiate for a better fit, only to be silenced by a glare. They quickly learned that in the army, they would have to accept what they were given and make it work.

The next station in their transformation was the barber – though 'butcher' might have been a more accurate description. The room was small and stark, with bare bulbs casting harsh light over three straight-backed wooden chairs. The floor was carpeted with hair of every colour.

Charlie watched, fascinated and horrified, as Harris – a young recruit who had only just been boasting about his sweetheart's love of his curls – stepped up to face his fate. The barber, a cadaverous man with nicotine-stained fingers, didn't waste time on pleasantries. With a few brutal swipes of his mechanical clippers, Harris' prized curls fell away in clumps, leaving his scalp exposed and vulnerable-looking under the merciless electric light.

By the time it was Charlie's turn, protest seemed futile. The hard wooden back of the chair pressed against his spine as the clippers came to life with a mechanical click. The vibration against his skull sent shivers down his neck, and he watched in the clouded mirror as tufts of his brown hair drifted down like dead leaves. The person staring back at him from the mirror became increasingly unfamiliar.

James, running a hand over his newly exposed scalp, grimaced at his reflection. "Blimey," he muttered. "Mother won't recognise me now."

Artie, ever the optimist, managed to find humour even in this transformation. "At least the lice won't like us," he quipped, rubbing his own bristly head with exaggerated satisfaction. "Though I suspect the girls back home won't much care for it either."

Charlie found himself chuckling, but the sound held little mirth. The reality of their situation was settling over them like an evening fog – thick, heavy, and impossible to ignore. Gone were the romantic notions of military glory that had filled their heads mere hours ago. There were no flags waving here, no cheering crowds, no brass bands playing patriotic tunes. Instead, there were only orders, movement, and the first harsh lessons in military discipline.

As dusk approached, they were marched to their barracks – a long wooden building that looked like it had been built more for utility than comfort. Inside, rows of thin metal bunks waited like iron sentinels, each with a thin mattress and two rough wool blankets. The air smelt of pine boards and something else – something that might have been fear, though none of them would have admitted it.

***

Dawn broke over the camp abruptly, the shrill blast of a whistle cutting through Charlie's dreams like a knife.

"Out of bed, you lazy sods!" The sergeant's voice carried the promise of consequences for any delay. "Five minutes to the parade ground!"

Before his mind had fully surfaced from sleep, before his eyes had even adjusted to the weak morning light filtering through the barracks' windows, Charlie found himself on his feet. His fingers, still clumsy with sleep, wrestled with buttons and laces as he donned his uniform, the rough wool scratching against his skin in what would become a familiar irritation.

The early morning air was cool but carried the promise of heat to come as they stumbled onto the parade ground. The rising sun cast a faint glow along the horizon, stretching long shadows across the ground.

Formation drill consumed the entire morning – left, right, left, right – an endless repetition that seemed designed to wear away the recruits' individuality. The sergeants' voices became a constant percussion, highlighting every misstep, every moment of hesitation, every failure to maintain perfect alignment.

"Straighten that line, Thompson!"

"For God's sake, Harris, your left! Your other left!"

"Pick up those feet, Greenly!"

By midday, they had progressed to what Sergeant Davies called "real soldier's work". The words sent a chill through Charlie despite the warm weather.

His pulse quickened as he watched the rifles being handed out, his heart seeming to skip several beats. A real rifle. Not a wooden training piece, not a toy from his childhood games, but a proper soldier's weapon. When one was finally thrust into his hands, the weight of it was staggering, a sensation somewhere between excitement and terror. It was heavier than he'd expected – the cold metal of the barrel and the solid wood of the stock combining into something that felt impossibly real in his grip.

"Mark well, boys," Sergeant Davies said, his voice taking on an almost reverent tone as he strode in front of them. He held up his own rifle, which gleamed in the light. "A Lee-Enfield rifle. Ten-round magazine. Standard issue for His Majesty's forces." He paused, letting his gaze sweep the line. "This..." he held the weapon at arm's length, as if presenting a holy relic, "...is your best friend. More than that, it's your lifeline. Your guardian angel. Your most faithful companion."

Several of the recruits shifted nervously, the gravel crunching beneath their boots.

The sergeant lowered the rifle, his expression hardening. "You will eat with it, sleep with it, train with it until it becomes an extension of your own body. You will know every scratch, every mark, every sound it makes. You will clean it until you can see your face in the metal, and then you will clean it again. If you drop it, if you neglect it, if you treat it with anything less than absolute respect, you will wish you'd dropped yourself instead."

Charlie could feel sweat beginning to form on his palms, making the wooden stock feel slippery in his grip.

"Now," Sergeant Davies continued, "you will learn to hold it, to clean it, to respect it. Because soon, very soon, you will be using it in battle. And when that moment comes, your life – and the lives of your fellow soldiers – will depend on how well you've learned these lessons."

Charlie's fingers tightened on the rifle stock until his knuckles turned white. The weight of the weapon seemed to grow with each word the sergeant spoke, as if the responsibility it represented was adding physical mass to the metal and wood.

This was real. This was actually happening. And soon he would have to use this rifle for its intended purpose. He would have to point it at another human being and pull the trigger.

The boy who had boarded the train just yesterday was already beginning to fade, like a photograph left too long in the sun. In his place, something else was emerging – something harder, something that would *need* to be harder to survive what was coming.

***

"Bayonets fixed!"

The command rang out across the training ground, and Charlie found himself moving with the others, his fingers finding the bayonet at his belt. The blade made a distinctive click as he slotted it onto his rifle. Before them stood a row of training dummies – rough humanoid shapes stuffed with straw and burlap, mounted on wooden posts driven deep into the ground. They swayed slightly in the light breeze, an unintentionally macabre dance that made Charlie wince.

"Now then," Sergeant Davies announced, his voice carrying across the assembled recruits. "A rifle will kill a man at a distance. It's clean, impersonal. You pull the trigger, and somewhere over there," he gestured vaguely at the horizon, "someone falls. But up close?" His voice dropped to a harsh growl that somehow carried to every ear. "Up close, it's the bayonet that does the work. And there's nothing clean about it."

He moved to one of the dummies with a predator's grace, his own weapon held at the ready. The movement was fluid, practiced, terrible in its efficiency. In one smooth motion, he lunged forward, driving the bayonet deep into the straw-filled target. The force of his thrust cracked through the wooden frame inside, the sound sharp and final.

Several of the men flinched visibly. Charlie felt his own stomach clench. This wasn't like the recruiting posters that had decorated the shop windows back home. This wasn't about looking smart in uniform or marching proudly through cheering crowds. This was about putting cold steel into another man's flesh and feeling the life leave him.

"Your turn," Sergeant Davies ordered, his voice brooking no argument as he withdrew his bayonet with a firm twist.

One by one, the recruits took their positions. Charlie watched as Artie stepped forward first, all traces of his usual cocky grin erased, replaced by a tight-lipped concentration that made him look like a stranger. The blade struck home with a solid thud, and Artie stepped back, his face slightly pale.

James followed, his jaw clenched so tight that Charlie could see the muscles working beneath his skin. His thrust was powerful but awkward, the bayonet catching in the burlap covering before tearing free.

Then it was Charlie's turn.

He stepped forward, feeling the eyes of his fellow recruits on his back. The weapon felt suddenly unwieldy in his hands, its familiar weight transformed into something strange and threatening. The dummy before him swayed gently, almost seeming to mock his hesitation.

He gripped the weapon tighter, trying to remember the proper stance they'd been shown, his feet searching for solid footing.

A second too long.

"Do it, Greenly!" Sergeant Davies' voice cracked like a whip across his consciousness. "The Hun won't wait for you to make up your mind! He won't stand there while you gather your courage! Strike, or be struck!"

Charlie inhaled sharply. In that moment, time seemed to stretch, and he could see everything with unusual clarity – the individual straws poking through the dummy's burlap skin, the way the clouds cast moving shadows across the parade ground.

Then he thrust the bayonet forward.

The blade struck home with a force that shook all the way up his arms, the impact jarring his shoulders. He could feel the resistance as the steel punched through burlap and straw, and the moment when it found the wooden post at the dummy's core.

He pulled it back, the movement requiring more effort than he'd expected. The blade emerged with a spray of straw, leaving behind a ragged hole that gaped like a wound.

His breath came in short, sharp bursts, and he realised he was shaking slightly. The reality of what this training represented hit him with the force of a physical blow. The enemy wouldn't be made of straw. They would be men, like him, with loved ones waiting for them somewhere. Men who would bleed and scream and die on his bayonet.

They were no longer playing at being soldiers. This was real now. This was war, and they were learning its terrible trade.

Chapter Six

The air reeked of damp earth, rot, and something worse – something metallic and cloying that clung to the back of Charlie's throat. It was the smell of rust, of oxidised metal, of blood both fresh and old that had seeped into the very soil of France. The stench had become as much a part of the landscape as the mud itself.

It had been mere hours since Charlie had left England's shores, but already the world of training camps and parade grounds felt like a half-remembered dream. The crisp uniforms, the polished brass, the orderly formations – they all belonged to another lifetime entirely. Now, the distant rumble of artillery fire felt surreal – a relentless drumbeat, an unseen storm on the horizon.

Charlie slid down into the trench, his hobnailed boots finding uncertain purchase on wooden duckboards that had long since surrendered to the endless moisture. The timber slats, worn smooth by countless feet, were treacherously slick beneath him.

His breath escaped in thick white plumes in the frigid morning air as he followed James and Artie through the narrow, winding trench system. The earthen walls loomed over them, a twisted maze reinforced with wooden beams and sandbags stacked in haphazard patterns that somehow held back the constant threat of collapse. Every few yards, the walls bore the scars of previous bombardments – hastily repaired sections where shells had torn away chunks of the parapet.

A sergeant approached – not Davies, but a new one – stepping carefully through the scattered soldiers, each busy with their own tasks. He was older, his face a map of deep lines carved by weather and worry, his eyes holding the hard wisdom of a man who had seen too much to be impressed by anything anymore.

"You're replacements," he muttered, his eyes sweeping over them. "Fresh from training, I take it?"

Charlie managed a nod, suddenly aware of how new his uniform must look despite the mud, how clean his rifle was compared to the battered weapons around him.

The sergeant snorted, a sound halfway between amusement and pity. "Green as spring grass, the lot of you." He jerked his chin further down the trench line, where the passage curved away into shadow. "Find yourselves a spot to settle. You'll be out there soon enough."

Charlie swallowed hard, his throat suddenly dry despite the damp air.

Out there.

Beyond the relative safety of the trench walls.

Beyond the final layer of sandbags that offered some pretence of protection.

He felt James nudge his arm, a gesture of reassurance that did little to calm the churning in his stomach. "Stick close to me, Charlie."

Charlie nodded, his fingers tightening around his rifle.

The constant sound of dripping water echoed through the trench like some maddening clock counting down to an unknown hour. The walls seemed to weep moisture, dark rivulets trickling down the packed earth between the wooden support beams. Every plank beneath Charlie's boots sank slightly with each step.

"Bloody hell," Artie muttered, adjusting his rifle strap for the hundredth time, his usual bravado cracking slightly around the edges. "It's worse than I imagined. All those training lectures didn't prepare us for this."

James remained silent, his eyes constantly moving, watching the veterans around them with an intensity that suggested he was trying to learn everything he could from their bearing, their movements, their very way of existing in this bizarre underground world. His expression remained carefully neutral, but Charlie could see the tension in his jaw.

Charlie followed his friend's gaze, taking in the tableau of trench life that surrounded them. The soldiers they'd been told about in training were now flesh and blood reality. Some sat hunched against the trench walls, smoking cigarettes with trembling hands and staring at nothing. Others cleaned their rifles with slow, mechanical movements, their hands working purely on muscle memory while their minds seemed to be somewhere far away – perhaps back home in England, or perhaps simply nowhere at all.

And then there were the ones who had passed beyond even that state – men who didn't move at all, who sat or stood with their heads bowed and their eyes empty, their faces the colour of chalk. They were the walking dead, men whose spirits had already departed even though their bodies continued to occupy space in the trench.

Charlie shuddered, wondering how long it would take before he began to look the same.

A large rat, fat from feasting on God-knew-what, scurried boldly between his boots and vanished into the mud without a trace. He had seen rats before, but something about this one made his skin crawl.

"Welcome to paradise, boys."

The voice made Charlie turn. A tall, broad-shouldered soldier stood nearby, his uniform bearing the marks of long service in the line. There was something about his bearing that suggested he'd been a labourer before the war.

"Luke Billings," the man introduced himself. "Been here for over a month now. Lucky me."

Charlie felt something cold settle in his chest, a weight that had nothing to do with the damp air or his sodden uniform.

Billings' expression was a blend of pity and resignation. "Get some rest if you can, lads. You'll need every scrap of it."

James frowned. "Oh?"

Billings gave him a knowing look – the kind that said he'd seen things they hadn't, things they wouldn't want to know even if he told them. "Because tomorrow, lads..." He exhaled heavily, rolling his shoulders as if trying to shed some invisible burden. "...you're going over the top."

The words hit Charlie like a physical blow, forcing the air from his lungs.

***

Despite his exhaustion, Charlie barely slept that night.

The trench never truly fell silent – even in the darkest hours, there was a constant undercurrent of noise. The low murmur of voices drifted through the darkness – men on watch, others writing letters home by the dim light of carefully shielded candles, some simply talking to keep the shadows at bay. Somewhere further down the line, a man coughed violently, the wet, rattling sound speaking of fever or worse. The sound echoed off the wooden walls until it seemed to come from everywhere at once.

Charlie lay on the hard wooden planks, his greatcoat wrapped tightly around his body like armour against both cold and fear. His rifle remained clutched close to his chest, the metal cold even through his uniform. He'd been taught to keep his weapon clean and close, but here that training took on new meaning. The rifle wasn't just a tool anymore – it was a lifeline, the only thing standing between him and whatever waited in the darkness beyond the parapet.

Tomorrow.

The word kept repeating in his head like a prayer, or perhaps a curse.

Tomorrow, he would leave the relative safety of these mud walls.

Tomorrow, he would face no man's land.

James lay next to him, close enough that Charlie could hear his measured breathing. Like Charlie, he stared up at the wooden beams above, where moisture gathered and dripped in an endless pattern. Then, in a whisper barely carrying over the ambient sounds of the trench, he spoke: "You awake?"

Charlie exhaled slowly, watching his breath form clouds in the frigid air. "Yes."

James turned his head slightly, and though his expression was difficult to read in the dim light, there was a vulnerability in his voice that Charlie had never heard before. "Think it'll be quick?"

Charlie hesitated, the question hanging between them. "I don't know."

Neither of them spoke for a long time, each

lost in their own thoughts of what "quick" might mean – quick victory, quick death, quick descent into the madness they'd seen in the eyes of the veterans.

Then Artie's voice came from the darkness, quiet but steady, carrying that hint of forced cheer he'd maintained since their days in basic training. "You're thinking too much."

Charlie glanced towards his friend's voice. Artie was lying back with his hands behind his head, adopting a pose of casual indifference that fooled none of them.

"Best not to dwell on it," Artie continued, as if reciting from some manual of soldierly behaviour. "We're here, we do our part, we go home. Simple as that."

James let out a breath that might have been a laugh under different circumstances. "That simple, is it?"

"Of course," Artie said firmly. "We're British, aren't we? King and Country and all that rot."

The words were meant as a joke, an echo of the patriotic fervour that had swept them all up back home, but the silence that followed was heavy with understanding. The weight of what awaited them tomorrow had stripped away those schoolboy fantasies, leaving only the cold reality of what they faced.

Charlie closed his eyes, trying to find some measure of rest, knowing he would need every ounce of strength for what lay ahead.

Tomorrow was coming, as inexorable as the tide.

***

Dawn arrived like a thief, creeping over the battlefield in a haze of grey light.

Charlie sat up stiffly, his limbs protesting every movement after hours spent on the unyielding duckboards. The cold had seeped deep into his muscles, making every motion an exercise in determination. Around him, the trench was already stirring to life – men moving efficiently, checking equipment, adjusting webbing, lighting cigarettes with trembling hands. Some knelt in corners, their lips moving in silent prayers, while others simply stared ahead with expressions that suggested they were already far away from this place.

"Up! Stand to!"

The command sent Charlie scrambling to his feet, his rifle already in hand, his body responding even as his mind raced with barely contained panic. He followed James and Artie to the fire step – a raised platform along the trench wall that would serve as their launching point into whatever hell awaited them.

Beyond the relative safety of the trench, no man's land stretched ahead – a barren, broken wasteland, more like something out of a nightmare than any terrain they had ever known. The ground was a chaos of mud and shell holes, cratered and torn by countless bombardments. Rusted barbed wire formed twisted patterns across the landscape, and here and there, half-submerged in the mire, lay the dark shapes of bodies. Some were recent additions to this charnel ground, while others had become part of the scenery itself, their uniforms rotting into the earth that had claimed them. Charlie forced himself not to look too closely at these grim landmarks, knowing that soon enough he would have to cross this horrific ground.

The sergeant appeared along the line, his face set in its customary grim expression, though Charlie thought he detected something else there now – a flicker of concern, perhaps, or resignation.

"Fix bayonets!"

Charlie swallowed hard but obeyed, sliding the long blade onto the end of his rifle with hands that he fought to keep steady. The metallic click of bayonets locking into place sounded up and down the line, a sound that transformed every rifle into a weapon of intimate killing.

A captain strode through the ranks, his uniform somehow maintaining a semblance of military precision that seemed almost obscene compared to the mud-caked soldiers around him. His polished boots and pristine Sam Browne belt marked him as someone who had likely arrived recently from headquarters, someone who hadn't yet been baptised in the mud and blood of the trenches.

"Men," he called out, his voice carrying the cultured accent of England's upper class, "today, we push forward! The Germans are weak! Their lines are thinning, and today we will break them! Today, we will have victory!"

The men remained silent, their faces masks of stone. Charlie's fingers tightened around his rifle stock until the wood creaked in protest. The weapon felt impossibly heavy now, weighted by his dread of what he would soon be required to do with it.

"One minute!" the captain ordered.

Charlie's heart hammered against his ribs with such force he was certain everyone around him could hear it.

All along the line, men prepared themselves in their own ways. Some crossed themselves with trembling fingers, others kissed lockets containing photographs of loved ones, while many simply muttered quiet goodbyes under their breath – to families, to friends, to the lives they'd left behind.

Artie turned to Charlie and James, his usual grin replaced by something fiercer, more primal. "Stick together," he said, his voice steady despite the fear that showed in his eyes. His hands gripped his rifle so tightly his knuckles showed white through the grime on his skin.

Charlie nodded, unable to find his voice. The simple act of breathing seemed to require all his concentration.

"Thirty seconds!"

"I thought I'd feel braver," James confessed.

Somewhere nearby, a soldier doubled over and vomited into the mud, the contents of his stomach joining the detritus of war that already filled the trench bottom. No one commented or even seemed to notice.

Another man was muttering to himself, the words becoming a desperate mantra: "Just a step forward. Just a step. Just one bloody step at a time."

"Ten seconds!"

Charlie's breath came in short, sharp gasps that didn't seem to provide enough air to his burning lungs.

A whistle screamed through the air like a banshee's wail.

"Over the top! GO! GO! GO!"

Charlie clambered up the trench ladder, his boots slipping on the damp wood that countless others had climbed before him. His webbing caught on a loose nail, and for one terrifying moment he thought he would be trapped there, suspended between earth and sky, but then the strap gave way with a sharp snap and he was moving again.

The moment he found himself above the parapet, the world erupted into an inferno of destruction beyond belief. The terrifying frenzy of war became an overwhelming assault on his senses.

Gunfire ripped through the air in endless waves. The sharp cracks of individual rifles were all but drowned beneath the mechanical stuttering roar of German machine guns – the sound veterans had grimly nicknamed the "Devil's Typewriter". Shells shrieked overhead like damned souls, exploding in tremendous bursts of fire and shattered earth that sent deadly fragments scything through the air.

Men spilled out of the trench all along the line, some leaping over tangles of barbed wire with desperate grace, others already falling – cut down before they'd taken more than a few steps into no man's land. Their bodies joined the others that littered the churned earth, fresh sacrifices to the hungry ground.

Charlie ran, his boots sinking into the thick, sucking mud with every step. The weight of his equipment seemed to drag at him like hands trying to pull him down into the earth. James was beside him, keeping pace stride for stride, while Artie pushed slightly ahead, his legs carrying him forward with desperate speed. Their faces were pale with naked fear but set with determination – the look of men who ran forward because the alternative was unthinkable.

A man to Charlie's right was struck mid-stride – his chest erupting in a spray of red mist as German bullets found their mark. The soldier crumpled without a sound, folding into the mire as if the earth had reached up to embrace him.

Charlie didn't stop. He couldn't stop.

They reached a stretch of barbed wire, a rusted barrier that seemed to grow up from the earth like some metallic species of weed. Men hunched over it with wire cutters, their hands shaking as they struggled to cut paths through the deadly mesh. Others attempted to climb over, their uniforms catching and tearing on the cruel barbs, leaving strips of cloth and sometimes flesh behind. The wire seemed alive, grasping and clawing at anything that tried to pass.

A shell hit the ground no more than twenty yards to Charlie's left, and the force of the explosion threw him off his feet as if he was nothing more than a child's toy. He hit the mud hard, the impact forcing the air from his lungs in a sharp, explosive gasp. His rifle flew from his grasp, disappearing into the churned earth nearby.

For a moment, all was ringing silence, as if the world itself had been stunned by the blast. The battlefield continued its deadly dance around him, but Charlie could hear nothing except a high-pitched whine that seemed to fill his entire skull. His vision swam, the grey sky above him spinning like a cursed carousel.

Then James appeared, materialising out of the smoke and chaos like a guardian angel in mud-caked khaki. His mouth moved, shouting something Charlie couldn't hear over the ringing in his ears. Grabbing Charlie's webbing with desperate strength, James hauled him to his feet. He thrust Charlie's rifle back into his hands and shoved him forward.

Gradually, sound began to return, filtering through the ringing in Charlie's ears like water through sand. The cacophony of battle crashed back over him in waves: the thunder of artillery, the constant crack of rifle fire, the screams of the wounded and dying.

They pressed on through the maelstrom, German gunfire kicking up fountains of mud around them. Each step felt like an eternity, each yard gained paid for in sweat and blood and desperate prayer. Artie had somehow maintained his lead, pushing forward with single-minded determination. He reached the next trench – the German line – and disappeared over the edge.

Charlie followed, his boots finding purchase on the lip of the enemy trench. He grabbed the top with mud-slicked hands and threw himself over, gravity taking hold and pulling him down into what felt like the bowels of hell itself.

The German trench was a charnel house, a nightmare realm of blood and chaos. The relatively ordered world of their own trench seemed a distant memory compared to this place of desperate, intimate combat. German soldiers fought with everything they had – bayonets, pistols, entrenching tools, fists – anything that might give them an edge in the close confines of the trench.

Artie was already locked in a life-or-death struggle mere yards away, his rifle knocked from his grip as a German soldier – little more than a boy, really – lunged at him with a knife.

Charlie didn't think – there was no time for thought, no space for hesitation. Training and instinct took over. He drove his bayonet forward with all his strength, feeling the resistance as the blade met flesh, the sharp jolt travelling up his arms as it found its mark. The action was almost surgical in its simplicity, yet nothing in his training had prepared him for the reality of it – the way it felt to drive steel into living flesh, to feel the life drain from another human being.

The German soldier let out a strangled sound, more surprise than pain, his eyes going wide with shock. His mouth opened as if to speak, but no words came. For a brief moment, their eyes met, and Charlie saw something there that would haunt him for the rest of his days – recognition, perhaps, or accusation, or simply the universal humanity that bound them both.

Charlie yanked the blade free with a motion that felt both necessary and obscene. His hands were shaking so badly he could barely maintain his grip on the weapon.

The German soldier collapsed at his feet, crumpling like a puppet whose strings had been cut. His body joined the others that already littered the trench floor, indistinguishable now from friend or foe.

Artie scrambled to reclaim his rifle, his breath coming in ragged gasps, his eyes flicking rapidly between Charlie and the body at their feet. His face was a mask of shock and something else – acknowledgement, maybe, of what they had all become in this dire place.

Neither of them spoke. There were no words adequate to the moment, no way to articulate the transformation that had just occurred. They were different men now than they had been mere minutes ago, changed in ways that could never be undone.

More men poured into the trench, the fighting still raging with undiminished fury. The narrow space was a crucible of violence, a place where civilisation's thin veneer had been stripped away to reveal the raw animal that lurked beneath.

Charlie barely had a moment to register what he had done – the life he had taken, the line he had crossed – before the battle swallowed them whole once more, demanding every ounce of their attention simply to survive the next moment, and the next, and the next.

Chapter Seven

The kitchen was filled with the comforting aroma of freshly baked bread and rich, simmering broth, but even these familiar scents, which had once brought such warmth and joy to the household, now seemed to emphasise the crushing emptiness that permeated every corner of the modest home. The late afternoon sunlight filtered through the lace curtains, casting dappled shadows across the worn wooden floorboards, a gentle reminder of how time continued to march forward, relentless and unforgiving.

Mrs Greenly stood at the iron stove, methodically stirring the pot of hearty stew that would serve as their evening meal. Her movements were slow and deliberate, each turn of the wooden spoon creating gentle ripples in the thick broth. Across the sturdy oak table, Elisabeth and Mary sat in uncharacteristic silence, their hands folded properly in their laps, their usual cheerful chatter conspicuously absent.

The calendar on the wall marked the passing of months since Charlie had left, each crossed-out day feeling like another small wound to his mother's already aching heart. She remembered that morning with painful clarity – how proud he had stood, how his eyes had sparkled with determination and adventure. If only she had known then how the weight of his absence would settle over their home, smothering their joy and leaving only whispers of what once was.

Her gaze drifted to the empty chair at the table – Charlie's chair. She hadn't allowed anyone to sit there since his departure, not even when Cousin Margaret had visited with her brood of children last Sunday. The wooden seat stood as a silent sentinel, a physical reminder of the void in their lives that grew deeper with each passing day. Even the slight scuff marks on its legs, from where Charlie had always restlessly shuffled his feet during meals, seemed precious now.

She turned back to the pot with almost desperate haste, blinking rapidly to dispel the familiar sting of tears that threatened to spill over. The scrape of the spoon against the pot's bottom provided a welcome distraction from her thoughts.

The heavy tread of boots on the wooden floorboards announced Mr Greenly's arrival before he appeared in the doorway. His tall frame filled the space as he entered, still wearing his work clothes, the smell of sawdust from the carpenter's shop clinging to his rough woollen jacket. Without a word, he took his customary place at the head of the table, unfolding *The Daily Telegraph*, as he did every evening. The newspaper had become both a blessing and a curse since Charlie had left – a potential source of news about the war, but also a bearer of lists they dreaded to read.

It was Mary who finally broke the silence, her small voice carrying the innocence of childhood. "When will Charlie come home?"

Mrs Greenly's hands stilled completely, the wooden spoon suspended above the pot as if frozen in time. The question they all carried in their hearts but dared not voice aloud had been laid bare by a child's simple enquiry.

Elisabeth, who had already learnt the careful dance of adult sensibilities, shot her younger sister a warning glance, but the damage was done. The question lingered in the air, demanding an answer that none of them could give.

Mr Greenly deliberately turned another page of his newspaper, his weathered face carefully arranged into an unreadable mask. The paper trembled slightly in his calloused hands, but if anyone noticed, they didn't mention it.

Mrs Greenly swallowed hard against the lump in her throat, gathering her strength before responding. "Soon, love," she said, forcing gentleness into her voice despite the ache in her chest. "Soon." The word felt hollow, a promise she had no power to keep.

Mary's brow furrowed in that particular way that reminded Mrs Greenly so much of Charlie when he was young and puzzling over his schoolwork. "But it's been so long," she persisted, her bottom lip quivering slightly. "Tommy Wilson's brother came home last week."

Mrs Greenly's hands clenched involuntarily around the wooden spoon. Tommy Wilson's brother had indeed come home – missing an arm. But she couldn't tell Mary that. Instead, she forced her features into what she hoped was a reassuring smile. "That just means Charlie's doing important work, love. Keeping us safe. Keeping all of England safe."

Mary nodded slowly, but her lip trembled more pronouncedly now. She looked down at her hands, her fingers twisting together in her lap like pale, restless birds.

Feeling guilty that she couldn't do more to comfort her daughter, Mrs Greenly turned back to the stove, her grip on the wooden spoon so tight her knuckles showed white beneath her skin. She would not cry. She could not cry. She had to be strong – for the girls, for her husband, for Charlie. Someone had to keep their world turning, even when it felt like it might shatter at any moment.

She lifted the heavy stew pot from the stove and carried it to the table. She ladled generous portions into each bowl, the rich aroma of beef and vegetables rising in steaming clouds. Charlie's place remained untouched, as it had every night since his departure. His bowl sat upturned on his plate, a small ritual of preservation that she couldn't bring herself to break.

Mr Greenly carefully folded his newspaper and set it aside, his movements deliberate and measured. The headlines about the Western Front were carefully turned face-down, though Mrs Greenly had caught glimpses of words like "casualties" and "offensive" before they disappeared from view. He reached for his spoon, clearing his throat slightly.

The girls began to eat, though Elisabeth merely pushed her food around the bowl, creating endless patterns in the thick broth as her spoon made soft clinking sounds.

As the meal continued in its quiet rhythm, Mrs Greenly pushed her food around without really tasting it, her thoughts elsewhere. The grandfather clock in the hallway ticked steadily, its pendulum marking the slow passage of time.

A sudden knock at the door broke the monotony, sharp and insistent.

Mr Greenly looked up from his food, his brow furrowing in surprise. "Now who could that be?" he muttered, setting his spoon down and pushing back from the table.

He rose from his seat and moved towards the door with slow but purposeful steps. The family could hear the faint shuffle of his boots on the floorboards as he reached for the handle.

As the door creaked open, standing on the doorstep was Mrs Bennett, the neighbour from two doors down. She was holding an envelope in her hands. It looked well-worn, its corners bent from the journey.

"Good evening, Mr Greenly," Mrs Bennett said, offering a polite smile despite the concern in her eyes. "I'm terribly sorry to trouble you, but I think this was delivered to our house by mistake."

Mr Greenly's gaze dropped to the envelope, his heart sinking at the sight of the military postmark. Without a word, he reached out and took it from her. "Thank you, Mrs Bennett," he said, his voice tight with gratitude.

The neighbour gave a slight nod before turning and walking back down the path, leaving Mr Greenly to close the door with a quiet click.

With the letter still in his hands, Mr Greenly stood for a moment in the hallway, staring at the envelope as if it might contain more than just ink on paper. Walking back to the dining table, his eyes met his wife's. Her face had gone pale.

"Is it from Charlie?" Mary asked, suddenly animated. Her eyes shone with the pure, uncomplicated joy that only children could still muster in the circumstances.

Mrs Greenly trembled as her husband handed her the letter and then sat back down at the table. Her fingers fumbled slightly as she extracted the precious pages from their envelope. The paper was thin and slightly crumpled, but covered in Charlie's familiar handwriting. The sight of those well-known loops and curves, so distinctly his own, brought tears to her eyes that she quickly blinked away.

She swallowed hard against the emotion threatening to overwhelm her and began to read aloud, her voice wavering only slightly:

"Dear Mum and Dad, Elisabeth and Mary,

I am well and in good spirits. The training was hard work, but I am learning quickly – quicker than most, the sergeant says. The men here are good sorts, solid chaps who look out for each other like brothers. We've formed quite a tight-knit group, sharing whatever comforts we can find. The food isn't a patch on yours, Mum, but we manage well enough with what we're given. James Cooper is here with me, and he sends his warmest regards to everyone back home.

Please don't worry yourselves about me. I promise to write again as soon as I can.

Love,
Charlie."

The room fell into a silence so profound that Mrs Greenly could hear the soft sputter of the oil lamp on the sideboard. Her eyes remained fixed on the letter, reading and re-reading each carefully penned word, searching for hidden meanings between the lines.

There was no mention of the war itself, no hint of the conditions they'd read about in the newspapers, no trace of fear or uncertainty. Just assurances and careful omissions. The censor's stamp seemed to mock her, a reminder of all the things her son couldn't – or wouldn't – tell them.

With her fingers still trembling, Mrs Greenly folded the letter along its well-worn creases and pressed it against her chest, as if she could somehow absorb its essence, feel some connection to her boy through the paper he had touched.

"He sounds well," she murmured, more to herself than to the others.

Elisabeth watched her mother's face intently. In many ways, she had grown up too quickly these past few months, shouldering burdens no child should have to bear. "Do you believe him?" she asked softly, the question carrying more weight than its simple words suggested.

Mrs Greenly's fingers tightened around the letter, the paper crinkling slightly under her grip. She forced her lips into what she hoped was a convincing smile, though it felt brittle as dried leaves.

"Of course," she said, with a certainty she didn't feel.

The lie tasted bitter on her tongue, but she told herself it was necessary – yet another sacrifice dictated by the war.

***

Later that evening, the house felt particularly empty, as if Charlie's words had somehow emphasised the space he should have occupied.

After the dishes had been cleared away, Mr Greenly settled into his worn leather armchair by the fire, his pipe cupped in one weathered hand. The tobacco smoke curled up towards the ceiling in lazy spirals as he stared into the dancing flames, his expression distant. He hadn't said more than a handful of words since they'd read Charlie's letter, though that wasn't unusual these days. He'd never been a man of many words, but since Charlie's departure, his silence had taken on a different quality – heavier, more pregnant with unspoken thoughts.

Mrs Greenly moved about the kitchen with mechanical efficiency, her hands performing the familiar evening tasks while her mind wandered far away. She could almost hear Charlie's laughter echoing from the garden, could almost see him bursting through the door with muddy boots and tousled hair, full of stories about his day at school or his adventures with the other boys in the town.

Elisabeth and Mary sat cross-legged on the hearth rug, engaged in a subdued game of cat's cradle with a length of worn yarn. Their usual giggles and playful squabbles were absent, replaced by an almost solemn concentration.

The shared silence seemed to press down on them all, as if Charlie's absence had finally materialised into something tangible, something that filled every corner of their home with its heavy presence.

It was Mary who finally spoke, her small voice cutting through the quiet. "Can we go into

Charlie's room?" she asked, looking up at her mother with those wide, innocent eyes.

Mrs Greenly's breath caught in her throat, and the teacup she was drying nearly slipped from her fingers. She set it down with deliberate care, trying to hide the tremor in her hands.

"No, love," she said, her voice gentle but firm, brooking no argument.

Mary's face crumpled into a frown, her lower lip jutting out slightly. "But why not? It's just a room," she persisted with the skewed logic of childhood. "All his things are getting dusty."

Elisabeth shot her younger sister a warning glance, sharp enough to cut, but the question had already been asked, hanging in the air, waiting for an answer.

Mrs Greenly turned slowly from the sink, wiping her hands methodically on her apron. The movement gave her a moment to compose herself. She looked tired – more than tired. There was a bone-deep weariness etched into the lines around her eyes, the kind that no amount of sleep could cure.

"Because it's Charlie's," she said softly, each word measured and careful, "and it'll be just as he left it when he comes home." She didn't add that she couldn't bear to see his room now – the perfectly made bed, the stack of books on his nightstand, the cricket bat leaning in the corner. Each item was a reminder of the life that had been interrupted, of the boy who had walked out of that room one morning and into a war that seemed to devour young men whole.

Mr Greenly cleared his throat, speaking for the first time in a while. "Best to leave it be," he said quietly. There was an unusual gentleness beneath his customary gruffness, a softness that spoke volumes about his own private grief. His pipe had gone cold in his hands, forgotten as he stared into the dying fire.

Mary nodded slowly, accepting this adult logic even if she didn't fully understand it. But Elisabeth remained still, her eyes fixed on her mother with an intensity that was almost uncomfortable.

The grandfather clock in the hallway began to toll the hour, its deep, resonant chimes echoing through the quiet house. Eight hollow notes that seemed to stretch endlessly.

Mrs Greenly clutched Charlie's letter again. As she read it to herself, she sensed the words were carefully chosen. She let out a slow, shaky breath, her fingers tracing the familiar loops and curves of his handwriting. How many times had she seen these same letters on his school essays, on hastily scribbled notes left on the kitchen table, on birthday cards made with childish care? Now each stroke of his pen was precious, a tangible connection to her son somewhere across the Channel.

She had seen the newspapers in town, tried to avoid looking at them but found her eyes drawn to their bold headlines and lengthy columns. The lists of names grew longer each week – sons and husbands and brothers who would never return home. The recruitment posters papered every available surface, their bright colours and stirring slogans a stark contrast to the growing shadow of grief that hung over the town. Other posters, aimed at women like her, urged patience and fortitude, speaking of duty and pride and sacrifice. As if they could wrap the agony of waiting in patriotic bunting and make it easier to bear.

But waiting was its own kind of torture – a slow, grinding pain that wore away at the soul. Each morning brought the same questions: Was Charlie warm enough? Had he eaten? Was he safe? Questions that echoed in her mind with no answers, only the empty comfort of hope and prayer.

She felt a gentle tug at her sleeve, pulling her back from the edge of darker thoughts. Looking down, she found Mary standing beside her, her face upturned and clouded with cautious optimism.

"Will you read it again?" Mary asked softly, her small fingers still clutching at the worn fabric of her mother's sleeve.

Mrs Greenly hesitated for a moment. Then, with a quiet sigh, she smoothed the pages and began to read.

"Dear Mum and Dad, Elisabeth and Mary..." she recited again, her voice low and gentle. She read each word with deliberate care, as if

they needed to be savoured, to become a part of her.

By the time she had finished reading, Mrs Greenly could see that Mary was beginning to look sleepy. She carefully folded the letter and tucked it into her apron pocket before bending down to scoop her daughter into her arms. The child was getting almost too big for this, but Mrs Greenly needed the comfort of holding her close as much as Mary needed to be held. She breathed in the clean, sweet scent of her daughter's hair, remembering how Charlie had smelt at this age – of sunshine and grass and mischief.

As she carried Mary up the stairs to bed, she whispered, "Sleep well, my love," her lips brushing against her daughter's forehead. Mary's head rested trustingly against her shoulder, her breathing already evening out into the peaceful rhythm of sleep.

When she reached the landing, Mrs Greenly allowed herself to close her eyes – if only for a moment. In the darkness behind her eyelids, she could pretend that Charlie was in his room, that the war was nothing but a bad dream, that their family was whole and safe and together.

Chapter Eight

Charlie couldn't feel his feet anymore – hadn't felt them properly for what seemed like an eternity. They had been submerged for days in the frigid, stagnant trench water, a murky soup of mud, blood, and God knew what else. Now they felt like leaden blocks of ice fused to his legs, unfamiliar appendages that no longer belonged to him. He attempted to wiggle his toes inside his waterlogged boots, but it was a futile gesture – the numbness had crept so deep into his bones that he wondered if he would ever feel warmth again.

The misery of it wasn't his alone. Every man who stood shoulder to shoulder in this godforsaken ditch was suffering in the same stoic silence, their faces mask-like in the grey dawn light, each lost in his own private hell.

The trench was thick with an unholy cocktail of stenches – rotting sandbags, damp earth that hadn't seen sunlight in months, unwashed bodies crammed together like cattle, and the sickly-sweet undertone of gangrene that no one dared mention. Somewhere further down the line, a man's violent coughing echoed off the muddy walls, the sound wet and ragged, like something essential was tearing loose inside him. Trench fever, Charlie knew. It spread like wildfire in conditions like this, passing from man to man as surely as their shared cigarettes and whispered fears.

Charlie adjusted his white-knuckled grip on his rifle, desperately trying to focus on anything but the crushing weight of their collective misery. The weapon's wooden stock was slick with the constant drizzle, and he could feel the metal parts beginning to rust despite his daily efforts to keep it clean. The rifle was his lifeline, his only constant in this maze of mud and death, and he treated it with more care than he showed his own body.

The rain fell steadily, adding to the filthy sludge beneath. Fat rats, bold as brass, skittered between the men's legs. The vermin had grown fat on things Charlie forced from his mind whenever he saw them scurrying past, their whiskers twitching with ghoulish satisfaction.

James sat beside him on a half-rotted firing step, his steel helmet tilted forward at an angle that almost hid his face. His eyes were closed, but Charlie knew he wasn't sleeping. No one truly slept in this hell – they just drifted in and out of an exhausted haze, always alert for the whistle that would send them scrambling, perhaps to their deaths.

Artie was stationed on Charlie's other side, his lips moving in an endless stream of barely audible muttering. His dirt-encrusted fingers traced and retraced the dented edge of a cigarette tin that had seen better days. Perhaps it was a lucky charm, or maybe just something solid to hold onto in a world where everything else seemed to be dissolving into mud and memory.

A voice drifted out of the shadows, small and uncertain, like a child's question in church.

"We'll be out of here soon, won't we? They promised we'd be home by Christmas."

Charlie turned his head slightly, just enough to catch sight of the speaker. The question had come from Edward Kearns, one of the new recruits who had arrived last week to replace the men lost in the last push. His face was still too soft for war, his cheeks somehow maintaining their roundness despite the meagre rations. He couldn't have been more than sixteen, though he'd surely lied about his age to enlist, as so many had.

No one answered immediately. The silence stretched out, growing more painful with each passing second.

Finally, James let out a long, weary breath. "Sure, lad," he muttered, his voice rough as sandpaper. "Soon enough."

Charlie tilted his head back, staring up at the narrow strip of sky visible above the trench walls. His body ached with an exhaustion that no amount of rest could cure, and his mind was too tired to even pretend to hope anymore. They had all stopped believing in "soon" months ago.

***

As the first weak light of dawn crept across the horizon, Charlie's body jerked upright before his mind had fully caught up, his muscles protesting even as they obeyed the instinct drilled into him by training. Around him, the men groaned as they forced stiff limbs into action, their faces tight with anticipation of what was to come.

The sergeant emerged from the half-light, moving down the line with the practiced efficiency of a man who had done this too many times before. "Stand to!" His voice was clipped, leaving no room for hesitation.

Charlie's hands found their familiar positions on his rifle as he pulled himself onto the fire step, his boots slipping against the wooden slats. Pressing himself against the trench wall, he peered carefully over the parapet, scanning the bleak landscape beyond.

No man's land stretched before him, a wasteland of craters and broken earth, endless in the cold, grey light of dawn. Tangles of barbed wire twisted across the muddy expanse, and beyond that, somewhere in the rolling banks of mist, lay the German trenches. The enemy was out there, waiting, watching – probably going through the same morning ritual.

Charlie exhaled slowly through his nose, trying to steady the tremor in his hands. The morning stand-to was a ritual as old as the war itself – both sides would man their positions just before sunrise, expecting an attack that usually never came. It was a dance they performed every day, a ceremony of fear and readiness that had lost none of its power to terrify despite its familiarity.

Most days, nothing happened.

Most days.

James stood beside Charlie, his rifle held with the steady hands of a man who had done this too many times before. Artie was on his other flank, still muttering – perhaps a prayer to a God who had long since abandoned these killing fields, or maybe just another soldier's desperate bargaining with fate.

Then...

A sound.

Charlie's heart seemed to stop mid-beat, frozen in his chest like a hare caught in the open.

Gunfire. Distant at first – scattered shots snapping through the air. Then a sudden, rolling thunder of machine guns erupted from the German line.

Shouts rang out along the trench. A flare streaked into the sky, its ghostly light flickering against the shifting smoke. Then came the shells. They screamed overhead like banshees, arcing high before plunging down to tear the earth asunder. The impact shook the trench walls, sending clumps of mud raining down. Somewhere to Charlie's left, someone was yelling orders – maybe the sergeant, maybe just another terrified man trying to make himself heard over the chaos.

The air thickened instantly, obscured by smoke, pulverised dirt, and the sharp, metallic reek of fresh blood. It made Charlie's eyes water and his stomach lurch.

"TAKE COVER!"

The command barely registered before Charlie threw himself down, pressing his body into the trench wall as bullets ripped through the air above him. Wood splintered and flew as the German fire chewed through the trench's meagre defences, sending deadly slivers in all directions. The world had erupted into a maelstrom of horror that seemed to consume everything in its path.

To his right, a man's scream cut through the din – high, terrible, and abruptly silenced.

Charlie pressed himself deeper into the mud, his fingers clenched tightly around his rifle. Another shell found its mark closer to his position, the impact sending tremors through the earth. The explosion was so close that he could feel the heat of it on his face, even as dirt and debris rained down around him.

The trench walls shuddered ominously, timber groaning under the strain. Next to him, he could hear James coughing violently, choking on the thick dust that filled the air.

A voice rang out – the sergeant, somehow making himself heard above the din.

"GET READY!"

Charlie forced himself to move, every muscle screaming in protest as he pushed himself up from the mud. His heart was hammering so hard he thought it might burst from his chest.

There was nowhere to run, nowhere to hide, nothing to do but face what was coming and pray that somehow, some way, he would live to see another dawn.

His ears still rang from the shell blast, the sound reducing the world to a muffled, underwater cacophony. The ground continued to tremble beneath his feet, each impact sending vibrations through his bones. Through the rolling banks of cordite smoke and the stuttering muzzle flashes of machine guns, dark shapes began to materialise – human figures moving with desperate speed across no man's land, their rifles held before them like crosses in a macabre procession.

The Germans were charging.

The sergeant's voice cut through the chaos like a knife, sharp with command and barely contained fear. "STAND TO! OPEN FIRE!"

Trying to control his ragged breathing, Charlie pressed the wooden stock of his rifle against his shoulder. His hands trembled as he lined up his first shot through the iron sights, the world narrowing to a single point of focus. A German soldier burst through the fog like a ghost taking solid form – too close now, too real, too human. The man's face was visible in terrible clarity: young, scared, determined.

The trigger felt impossibly heavy under Charlie's finger.

But still he squeezed.

The rifle kicked hard against his shoulder, the familiar recoil almost comforting in its violence. Through the gun smoke, he saw the German soldier stumble mid-stride, his body contorting before crumpling into the churned earth of no man's land.

Charlie felt sick. He had hit him. He had *killed* him. Somewhere in Germany, a mother's son would never come home, and Charlie had made that happen with a single pull of his trigger.

But there was no time for the luxury of remorse.

More German soldiers came charging through the fog, their voices raised in guttural battle cries that sounded more terrified than fierce. Bullets whipped past Charlie's head with their distinctive crack-whine, close enough that he could feel the displacement of air against his skin.

James fired steadily beside him, his rifle's report blending into the cacophony of battle. His face was set in a granite mask of concentration, each shot delivered with mechanical precision. On Charlie's other side, Artie was reloading with frantic efficiency, his earlier prayers replaced by a steady stream of curses.

A small, dark object arced through the air, end over end, its trajectory burning itself into Charlie's vision.

"GRENADE!" The warning cry came too late.

"TAKE COVER!" someone screamed.

Charlie threw himself down just as the bomb exploded, the blast wave picking him up and throwing him backwards like a rag doll. For a terrifying moment, the world lost all sense of up or down. His vision blurred into a smear of grey and brown, and his ears filled with a high-pitched keening that drowned out everything else.

When his senses finally reasserted themselves, he found himself staring up at a sky he could barely see through the thick smoke. Bodies lay strewn across the trench, some moving, others terrifyingly still. The air was thick with the acrid smell of explosive residue and something worse – the copper-sweet stench of fresh blood and torn flesh.

And then...

The real horror began.

The Germans had reached the trench.

Charlie barely had time to register the looming figure above him before a bayonet flashed downward, aimed at his chest with killing intent. Pure instinct took over, and he rolled sideways, feeling the cold steel slice through his uniform sleeve and bite into the flesh beneath. Pain flared hot and immediate, but the wound was shallow – a graze rather than the mortal thrust it had been intended to be.

The German soldier's momentum carried him forward, throwing him slightly off balance. It was only a fraction of a second of vulnerability, but in the intimate violence of trench warfare, a fraction of a second was all that separated the living from the dead.

Charlie seized that moment, scrambling to his feet despite the slick mud threatening to drag him down. His boots slipped as he fought for balance, every muscle burning with the effort – but survival demanded speed.

Charlie didn't think. He couldn't afford to think.

He drove his bayonet forward with all the strength that fear and desperation could provide. The blade struck home, punching through the German's wool uniform and into the soft flesh beneath with terrible ease.

The soldier's eyes went wide with shock and pain – and something else, something that would haunt Charlie's nightmares forever. It was the look of a man realising that his story was ending, that all his hopes and dreams and fears were about to become meaningless.

Charlie twisted the bayonet, just as he'd been trained to do in those innocent days of basic training that now seemed like another lifetime. The motion was mechanical, automatic, learned by rote and executed without thought.

The German soldier collapsed, his body going slack.

Charlie staggered backwards, his breath coming in ragged gasps that tasted of copper and cordite. His hands were slick with blood – warm, sticky, and so terribly red against his pale skin.

The battle still raged around him, but for a moment, all he could do was stare at the body at his feet. Not a soldier anymore, not an enemy, just a body. A person he had killed with his own hands, close enough to feel their last breath.

His stomach heaved violently, and it took every ounce of his self-control not to vomit.

James' hand seized his shoulder, the grip firm enough to shock Charlie back to the present moment.

"Charlie! They're falling back!"

Charlie blinked hard, his mind struggling to process the words through the fog of shock and adrenaline.

The Germans were indeed retreating – scrambling back over the trench walls with the same desperate energy that had brought them forward. They dragged their wounded with them when they could, leaving their dead behind to keep company with the British corpses.

The fury of battle had faded, but the quiet that followed was worse – thick with the moans of the wounded, the rasping gasps of the dying, and the muffled sobs of men who had seen and done things no human being should ever have to endure.

Charlie's legs finally gave out beneath him, and he slumped against the trench wall, sliding down into the mud. He stared at his bloodied hands as if they belonged to someone else, turning them over in the weak morning light. The blood was already beginning to dry, turning brown and flaking away like rust.

Something fundamental had shifted inside him, some essential part of his soul had been irretrievably lost in the mud and chaos of the morning's battle. He felt hollow, as if everything that had made him who he was had been scooped out, leaving nothing but an empty shell in a mud-stained uniform.

The world had gone quiet, but it wasn't the kind of quiet Charlie remembered from home – not the peaceful stillness of dusk settling over his town, not the gentle hush that fell over the fields as the sun set, not the calming presence of his mother working in the kitchen as she prepared the evening meal. Those memories felt like echoes from another life.

A weak voice cut through his daze, barely more than a whisper from the trench floor.

"Help... please..."

Charlie turned his head slowly, his heart

lurching painfully in his chest as recognition dawned.

It was Edward Kearns – the same young recruit who had spoken so hopefully the night before, who had asked if they would be leaving the trenches soon, who had still believed in promises of home and better tomorrows. He lay crumpled against the mud wall, his uniform dark and wet with blood that pumped steadily from a wound in his abdomen. His hands clutched uselessly at the injury, trying to hold in what could not be contained, to fix what could not be mended.

Charlie crawled towards him, his knees slipping in the mud, his hands reaching out desperately without any real purpose. What could he do? What could anyone do?

Kearns' eyes met his – they were blue, Charlie noticed for the first time, bright blue like summer skies they hadn't seen in months. Those eyes were wide with terror now, filled with the desperate realisation that something was terribly, irreversibly wrong.

Charlie pressed his hands over the wound, but the blood wouldn't stop. It seeped between his fingers, hot and insistent, carrying Kearns' life away into the thirsty mud of the trench.

Kearns gasped, the sound wet and horrible. "Am I..." He coughed, bright red blood speckling his lips like macabre freckles. "... going home?"

Charlie opened his mouth, but no words would come. What could he say? What words could possibly matter now?

Kearns' breathing became more laboured, each breath a struggle against the inevitable. His grip on Charlie's wrist weakened, his fingers growing cold even as Charlie held them.

A moment later, his eyes went still, the bright blue dulling to the flat colour of an overcast sky. He stared upward, unseeing, another young soul taken by the war's insatiable appetite.

Charlie didn't move. He couldn't.

Someone exhaled sharply beside him – James, probably, though Charlie couldn't bring himself to look.

Artie's voice came from above, hollow and raw. "Bloody hell."

Charlie finally forced himself to sit back, his hands falling uselessly into his lap, red and slick and shaking. The blood was already beginning to dry, turning brown and crusty around his fingernails.

One moment, Kearns had been just a boy, full of hope and dreams and foolish questions about going home. A boy who probably still had his mother's last letter tucked safely in his breast pocket, who might have had a sweetheart waiting somewhere in England, who had likely lied about his age to join up because he believed in something greater than himself.

Now, he was just another body in the mud, another name to be written in a letter that would shatter a family's world, another cross to be planted in an endless row.

The rain began to fall again, a steady, miserable drizzle that seemed to mock their suffering. The drops mingled with the blood and filth in the trench. Nature itself was trying to wash away the evidence of what men had done to each other, but some stains, Charlie knew, would never truly fade.

Further down the line, a medic worked with frantic intensity on another wounded soldier, his hands slick with blood, his face set in an expression of exhausted determination. Charlie wondered if the medic still believed he could save everyone, or if he had come to accept that some would slip through his fingers no matter what he did.

In a corner of the trench, a soldier sat with his back against the wall, crying softly and whispering the same name over and over like a prayer or a curse. No one approached him. They all understood that some griefs needed to be borne alone.

The survivors moved through the aftermath like ghosts, their eyes vacant, their movements mechanical. No one spoke. What was there to say? Words seemed inadequate, almost obscene in the face of what they had witnessed, what they had done.

Charlie looked down at his clenched fists, at the blood that had dried into the creases of his knuckles. He had killed today, had watched the light fade from a man's eyes, had felt the resistance of flesh against his bayonet, had seen the moment when a human being became just another body in the mud. He had witnessed a boy's last breath, had felt the final desperate grip of fingers seeking comfort in their last moments.

And tomorrow...

Tomorrow, he would have to do it all over again. They all would. More men would die, and more blood would soak into the endless mud, and the war would grind on, insatiable, uncaring, eternal.

The rain continued to fall, washing away the blood but not the memory, never the memory. Charlie tilted his face up to the sky, letting the cold drops mingle with the tears he hadn't realised he was shedding.

Somewhere, in peaceful England, his mother was probably tending to her garden, praying for her son's safe return. He wondered if she would recognise the man who might eventually come home – if he came home at all.

The war had changed them all, had turned boys into killers, had transformed humans into numbers on a casualty list. And it wasn't finished with them yet.

Chapter Nine

Charlie stepped off the train onto the worn wooden platform of the station, and immediately the world around him seemed to shimmer like a mirage. Nothing felt real, as if he had wandered into someone else's dream rather than his own homecoming.

He was home. The word echoed in his mind, foreign and familiar all at once.

The station, once a grand fixture of his childhood memories, now seemed to have shrunk during his absence. The faces that moved around him were those of strangers – or perhaps he had become the stranger, transformed by years of warfare into someone these peaceful townsfolk could no longer recognise. He adjusted his grip on the leather strap of his military-issued bag, allowing it to dig into his shoulder. The sensation was grounding, a reminder that this wasn't another fever dream in a muddy dugout.

Officially, the war was over, though for him, it didn't feel like it.

The air here was wrong – too clean, too pure. It lacked the acrid bite of cordite, the metallic tang of blood, the perpetual reek of mud and unwashed bodies and death that had become as familiar as breathing. The absence of certain noises pressed against his ears like cotton wool, unsettling in its completeness. There were no distant artillery barrages, no urgent whistle blasts signalling yet another attack, no cries of suffering from the wounded and dying. The peace felt like a lie.

A small but eager crowd had gathered on the platform, families waiting with barely contained hope for their returning soldiers. Some would be reunited today. Others would wait forever, their loved ones lying in unmarked graves across the Channel, their bodies forever part of the foreign soil they had died defending.

Charlie saw his family before they noticed him.

His mother stood near the station's entrance, her hands clasped tightly in front of her. Her face was pale and drawn, but her eyes darted frantically across the platform, searching every uniformed figure with desperate intensity. His father stood beside her, ramrod straight as always, a man who had always believed actions spoke louder than words. But even from a distance, Charlie could see something in his father's eyes that he had never witnessed before – a vulnerability, a fear that perhaps their boy wouldn't be among those returning.

Elisabeth had grown impossibly tall in his absence, no longer the twelve-year-old girl he had left behind but a young woman with a quiet steadiness in her gaze. Beside her stood Mary, now ten, no longer the wide-eyed child he remembered. She clung to Elisabeth's hand, though more out of need than habit. It startled Charlie how much they had changed – how much he had missed. The war had stolen time from all of them, reshaping them in ways both subtle and profound.

Charlie forced himself to take a step forward. His mother's eyes finally found him, and for a long moment, she simply stared, as if she couldn't quite believe what she was seeing. As if she feared he might vanish if she blinked.

Then she ran to him, her shoes clattering against the platform boards, her composure shattering like glass. Her arms wrapped around him with desperate strength, her entire body shaking with deep, wracking sobs that seemed to come from her very soul. "Oh, Charlie... oh, my love... my boy... you're home... you're really home..."

He stood rigid in her embrace, his muscles locked in place, his lungs seemingly forgetting how to draw breath. The sensation of being touched without violence felt odd, wrong somehow. His body had forgotten the language of gentle contact.

Then, slowly – awkwardly – he raised one hand and rested it against his mother's back, feeling the sharp edges of her shoulder blades through her dress. She felt so small, so fragile in his arms. Had she always been this delicate, or had the war changed his perception of everything, even this?

His father stepped forward next, moving with careful deliberation. He was the same man Charlie remembered, yet profoundly different. More grey had crept into his hair at the temples, and deep lines had been carved into his face by worry and waiting. His hands, strong but weathered, hung uncertainly at his sides.

For a long, heavy moment, father and son simply looked at each other, measuring the changes time and war had wrought.

Then his father extended his hand, an offer of connection that somehow meant more than any embrace could have conveyed.

Charlie took it, noting how his own hand, once smaller than his father's, now matched it in size. The grip was firm, steady, grounding. But his father's eyes moved over him with careful attention – taking in his military bearing, the precise way he held himself, the shadows that lurked behind his eyes. Charlie could see the questions forming, the growing realisation that the son who had returned was not quite the same as the one who had left.

Charlie wondered if his father could see what he had become in the trenches. If he could read the toll of the killing in his eyes, sense the weight of the lives he had taken. He wondered if his father even recognised him anymore, or if he saw only a stranger wearing his son's face.

The walk home stretched longer than memory suggested it should, each familiar street somehow transformed into something simultaneously known and foreign. The terraced houses lining the way were exactly as he remembered, yet they seemed smaller now, diminished by his experiences of the wider world. Children played with carefree abandon, their laughter and shouts echoing off the buildings as they kicked a worn leather ball between them. They played as if nothing had changed, as if the world hadn't been torn apart and stitched back together, leaving ugly scars that would never fully heal.

Charlie's grip remained tight on his bag's strap, his polished boots scuffing against the familiar cobblestones. Each step felt like a negotiation between his past and present selves, neither quite willing to cede control.

His mother filled the silence with gentle, nervous chatter as they walked, touching on safe subjects while carefully avoiding the deeper waters of his absence.

"I've kept your room exactly as you left it," she said, her voice carrying a hint of pride mixed with uncertainty. "Everything's just waiting for you, love. Just as it was."

Charlie managed a nod but couldn't find his voice. How could he explain that the boy who had lived in that room was gone?

Their house came into view around the final bend in the lane, and Charlie felt his chest tighten. It stood exactly as it had in his dreams and memories, dark green ivy still climbing the old brick walls like nature's own tapestry. The front door's blue paint had faded slightly in his years away, but his mother's handmade lace curtains still hung in the windows – yellowed with age but kept pristine.

Standing before it now, Charlie felt nothing of the warmth or relief he had imagined during countless cold nights in the trenches. Instead, there was only a hollow emptiness, as though he was looking at a skilled painting of home rather than the place itself.

His mother turned to him, her face hopeful yet cautious, like someone approaching a wounded animal. "Come inside, love. Let's get you settled."

Charlie hesitated, suddenly acutely aware of his appearance. His boots, though recently cleaned, still carried traces of French mud in their creases. His uniform, despite his best efforts, remained creased and marked with stains he preferred not to identify. Standing on the threshold of this clean, peaceful home, he felt like a corruption, a dark presence threatening to taint this untouched space.

But his mother's hand found his arm, her touch gentle but insistent as she guided him forward. The gesture was so familiar, so maternal, that for a moment he felt like a child again, being led inside after falling and scraping his knee.

He stepped through the doorway.

The house's scent hit him immediately. Warm bread fresh from the oven, his mother's dried lavender hanging in bunches from the kitchen ceiling, the sweet smokiness of the hearth – all of it exactly as he remembered, exactly as he had dreamed of during his darkest moments. But somehow, it still felt hollow. The familiar scents and sights seemed to belong to someone else's life, someone else's memories. He felt like an intruder, a ghost haunting the halls of his own past.

His mother's smile remained bright, hopeful, expectant. "Everything's just as you left it, love. Why don't you get yourself settled? You can put your bag in your room."

Charlie hesitated for a moment, his grip tightening on the strap of his bag. Then, with a slow nod, he turned towards the stairs. His fingers cautiously traced the banister as he ascended. At the top of the staircase, he paused. The door to his bedroom stood just ahead – familiar, unchanged, yet somehow strange.

As he stood in the doorway of his bedroom, frozen between past and present, he noticed that true to his mother's word, everything remained exactly as he had left it that bright summer morning when he'd marched off to war with dreams of glory in his head. The bed was meticulously made, the woollen blanket folded neatly at its foot. His collection of books stood on the shelf just as he'd left them, their spines cracked and worn from countless readings. Some pages still bore folded corners, marking the exact spots where his younger self had last paused in his adventures.

The wooden toy soldier he'd carved under his father's patient guidance still maintained its post on the windowsill, though its once-bright paint had faded. Its small, detailed face still wore the same determined expression, the same naive courage that Charlie had once possessed himself.

Nothing had changed in this room. But everything had changed in him.

His mother hovered anxiously behind him. "Go on, love. It's your room. It's been waiting for you."

Charlie forced himself to step inside, wincing as the floorboards creaked beneath his boots – a sound so familiar it felt like a physical pain. He set his bag down by the door, but the simple action felt wrong, discordant, like a false note in a well-loved song. He felt like he was defiling this preserved shrine to his former self with his mere presence.

He should have felt something here – comfort, relief, the embrace of familiar surroundings. Instead, the walls seemed to press in around him, the air thick and heavy with expectations he could never fulfil.

His mother lingered in the doorway, watching him with careful attention, trying to determine if it was safe to approach. Her eyes caught every subtle movement, every tension in his shoulders, every moment of hesitation.

"Are you hungry?" she asked, her voice carrying forced brightness. "I could make something special. Your favourites, just like before – shepherd's pie, or maybe that rabbit stew you always loved?"

Charlie's throat tightened at the word. *Before.*

Before the trenches had become his home, before he had killed men whose only crime was being born on the other side of a line on a map, before friends had died in his arms, before he had learnt that glory was a lie sold to boys to make them into killers.

His stomach churned at the thought of food. The army's rations – hard biscuits and tinned beef – had been poor fare, but at least they hadn't carried the weight of memory, of everything he had lost.

"I'm fine, Mum," he managed, his voice sounding distant and hollow even to his own ears. "Really."

She hesitated, and he could see the words building behind her lips – questions about the war, about his experiences, about the shadows she surely saw in his eyes. But something in his posture must have warned her away.

She nodded, accepting the lie with maternal grace. "I'll leave you to settle in, then."

She lingered a moment longer, as if memorising him, before quietly closing the door behind her.

The moment she was gone, Charlie's carefully maintained posture crumbled. He sat heavily on the edge of his bed, his hands gripping his knees so tightly his knuckles went white. The springs creaked beneath him – another familiar sound that now felt wrong, out of place. He was home, surrounded by the artefacts of his former life. So why did he feel like an impostor, a shadow haunting the space of his own past?

The silence of the house pressed against him like a physical weight. No distant thunder of artillery. No scurrying of trench rats seeking scraps of food or flesh. No wet coughs of men drowning in their own lungs from gas attacks, no whispered prayers, no muffled sobs in the darkness. Just silence, heavy and expectant, waiting for him to become the boy he had been before.

His fingers twitched with the need for a cigarette, a habit he'd picked up in the trenches where tobacco had been as valuable as ammunition. The familiar ritual of rolling a cigarette had been one of the few moments of normality in the chaos, a reason to keep his hands steady when the world was shaking apart around him. But he had none left.

Besides, his mother would be scandalised by the habit. Another piece of his war-self that didn't fit in this peaceful world.

His mind wandered, an involuntary pull he couldn't seem to fight. His thoughts drifted to James. He closed his eyes, but it only made the memories sharper. He had held his dear friend until the end, until the last breath had rattled from his chest, until his body had gone cold in his arms.

He had promised to write to James' mother, to tell her how her son had died a hero's death. But the letter remained unwritten, the words refusing to come. How could he tell her that her boy had died choking on his own blood in a muddy ditch in France? That his last words hadn't been of home or country, but a desperate plea for his mother as his life drained away?

A floorboard creaked in the hallway outside his room, and Charlie's body reacted before his mind could catch up. His muscles tensed, ready to dive for cover, his hands reaching automatically for a rifle that wasn't there. His heart hammered in his chest as adrenaline flooded his system, preparing him for an attack that wouldn't come.

It was just someone in the hallway, walking peacefully along, going about their quiet, unremarkable day.

Charlie forced himself to exhale slowly, deliberately, the way the medical officers had taught them to manage the shell shock. He was home. He was safe. The war was over. But part of him was still there, and always would be.

****

The morning light crept through his window like a cautious visitor, painting golden streaks across the wooden floor. Charlie watched them move with the detached interest of someone who had spent countless hours observing the play of light and shadow, seeking patterns in them to stay sane.

He hadn't slept. Instead, he had spent the night marking time by the familiar sounds of the house – the settling of old timbers, the soft creak of floorboards contracting in the cool night air, the distant chime of the church clock marking the hours.

A gentle knock at his door sent his heart racing again, his body tensing for action before his mind could assert control.

The door opened slowly, carefully, and his mother's face appeared in the gap, wearing a hesitant smile that didn't quite reach her eyes.

"Morning, love," she said softly, as if afraid to break the fragile peace of dawn. "I wasn't sure whether to wake you, but breakfast is ready. I've made your favourite – eggs and bacon."

Charlie ran a hand over his face, feeling the rough stubble that had grown overnight. "Thank you, Mum. I'll be down in a minute."

She lingered in the doorway, and he could see the words forming behind her eyes – questions about his sleepless night, about the shadows under his eyes that spoke of countless such nights. Despite this, she simply nodded, accepting his words at face value. "Take your time, love. There's no rush."

She closed the door with the same careful gentleness, leaving him alone with his thoughts once more.

Charlie swung his legs over the side of the bed, his feet finding the cool wooden floor, but he didn't move to dress. Not yet.

For the first time since stepping off the train, he allowed himself to consider what came next. Before the war, his life had stretched before him like a well-marked path. He would have followed in his father's footsteps, working in the town, perhaps taking up a trade. He would have married a local girl – maybe Sarah from the bakery, who had always smiled so sweetly at him. They would have had children, watched them grow, lived out their days in the peaceful rhythm of a quiet life.

But now? He wasn't sure who he was anymore, let alone what he should do with whatever remained of his life.

The war had taken something from him – something vital and irreplaceable. His youth, certainly. His innocence, without question. But more than that, it had taken his sense of purpose, his understanding of his place in the world. He had been a soldier, and a good one. He had learned to kill efficiently, to follow orders without question, to suppress his humanity when necessary for survival.

What did a soldier do when there was no war left to fight? When the skills that had kept him alive for years became useless overnight?

Who was he now?

Chapter Ten

The garden of the grand stately home stretched out before Charlie in the warm afternoon light of late summer 1973. Kept immaculate by the groundskeepers, it had been chosen by Thames Television as the perfect filming location. The air hung heavy with the perfume of roses and freshly cut grass, punctuated only by the gentle chorus of wood pigeons cooing in the oak trees and the occasional whisper of wind through the precisely trimmed yew hedges.

He sat in a sturdy wooden chair that had been carefully positioned by the production crew, his posture remaining as disciplined as it had been during his military service nearly sixty years prior. Though his hair had long since turned a stark white and his frame had grown leaner with the passing decades, he maintained a quiet dignity that spoke of his generation – one that had witnessed the world transform from horse-drawn carriages to colour television and men walking on the moon.

Across from Charlie, the interviewer from Thames Television's documentary unit adjusted his lapel microphone. He was a much younger man, though his earnest demeanour and freshly pressed brown suit made him appear older. Around them, the film crew moved with deliberate care, positioning reflectors to tame the shifting afternoon light, checking sound levels, and ensuring the camera was loaded with fresh film stock.

"Are you quite comfortable, Mr Greenly?" the interviewer asked, his clipped received pronunciation making each word crisp. "We can fetch another cushion if you'd like."

Charlie offered a small, reassuring smile. "I'm quite comfortable, thank you. These old bones have sat through worse than a garden chair."

The interviewer nodded, shuffling through his meticulously prepared notes before settling on his opening page. The papers rustled softly in the gentle breeze. "First and foremost, I want to express our profound gratitude for your willingness to speak with us today. With the passing years, it becomes increasingly vital to preserve these first-hand accounts. To hear directly from those who lived through such momentous events."

Charlie studied the younger man's face, noting the genuine respect in his expression. Though his words were well-meant, they stirred memories Charlie usually kept carefully locked away. Some days, the fact that he'd survived felt less like a triumph and more like a peculiar kind of haunting. It was as if his true self had been left behind in some muddy trench in France, and the decades since had been nothing more than an elaborate performance of living.

Still, he nodded, his weathered hands resting lightly on his knees. "Indeed, It's best that people remember. Especially now, with all these new wars brewing. Vietnam and the like."

The interviewer smiled encouragingly. The cameraman gave a subtle signal that they were rolling. "Let's begin at the start, shall we? You enlisted in 1914?"

Charlie drew in a measured breath, the sweet scent of nearby lavender momentarily transporting him back to his mother's garden. "That's right. I lied about my age, like plenty of lads did. I told them I was eighteen, but I was fifteen really. The recruitment sergeant must have known, mind you, but they weren't exactly checking too carefully in those days."

"And what was it like, back then? What was the mood of the country?"

Charlie's gaze drifted past the interviewer, beyond the carefully manicured lawn with its neat borders of Canterbury bells and delphinium, to somewhere far more distant in both time and space. The world had kept turning, had rebuilt itself again and again, yet here he sat, still carrying the weight of those years like a stone in his chest.

He considered how to capture it – the electric excitement that had coursed through the streets, the brass band playing in the town square, the way young men had practically tripped over themselves rushing to the recruitment office. How could he explain to this generation, raised in the shadow of the Second World War, the naive certainty they'd all shared that their war would be different, glorious, quick?

He looked back at the interviewer, noting how the young man's fingers rested expectantly on the edge of his notes. "It was a different time entirely," he said finally. "We were all so certain we knew what war meant. Thought it would be like the stories we'd read – gallant charges, heroic victories, home in time for Christmas dinner with a medal on your chest."

The camera whirred softly in the background as the interviewer leaned forward slightly. "Did you believe in what you were fighting for? The cause itself?"

Charlie's fingers tightened almost imperceptibly against the fabric of his trousers, the material well-worn but immaculately pressed – old habits died hard, after all.

Did he believe? Back then, absolutely. The righteousness of it had seemed so clear, so simple. King and Country. Standing up to the Kaiser's aggression. Now, after everything he'd seen, after watching an entire generation feed itself into the grind of industrial warfare... now he wasn't so sure of anything anymore.

Charlie took another deep breath, his eyes fixed on a point just beyond the television crew, where a robin was pecking at the manicured lawn. "Back then," he said carefully, choosing each word with deliberate precision, "we thought it was the right thing. The only thing. The newspapers were full of it – German atrocities in Belgium, the call to arms, our duty to civilisation. We thought we'd be home by Christmas, every last one of us. Thought it would be an adventure."

The interviewer nodded encouragingly. "And when did you realise that wouldn't be the case? That this war would be different?"

Charlie exhaled slowly through his nose, his fingers curling slightly against his leg as remembered sensations washed over him – the weight of wet wool, the perpetual cold, the peculiar metallic taste in the back of his throat.

"It's not something you can pin down to a single moment," he said finally, his voice steady despite the tremor in his hands. "It creeps up on you, like a fog rolling in. First it's the mud, then the shells that never seem to stop. Time becomes strange out there. Every second feels like an eternity when you're huddled in a trench, waiting for the whistle, but somehow months slip by without you noticing."

Charlie noticed that even the birds had fallen silent, as if nature itself was holding its breath to hear what came next. Despite the peaceful garden before him, however, his mind drifted to something else entirely, something buried beneath nearly six decades of carefully constructed normalcy.

"I still remember the lads," he continued, his words wavering slightly with emotion. "Tommy Newman. Barely seventeen, though he'd told them he was nineteen. Had a shock of red hair. He used to write to his mum every Sunday without fail, even when we were in the thick of it. Asked me once, in the autumn of fifteen, if I thought we'd be home soon."

A heavy silence settled over the garden. Even

the film crew had grown still, their equipment forgotten for a moment.

"What happened to him?" the interviewer asked, his voice barely above a whisper, though the microphone would catch every word.

Charlie's jaw tightened perceptibly. He had shared war stories before, of course – in pub corners with other veterans who understood, in letters to old comrades, even to Margaret in the early years of their marriage, before they'd silently agreed that some ghosts were better left undisturbed. But this was different. This wasn't just remembering; this was testimony. This would be preserved in the archives of Thames Television, perhaps shown to schoolchildren who couldn't begin to comprehend what it had been like, to historians trying to understand a war that had reshaped the world.

And maybe that was precisely why he needed to say it. Maybe that was why he had finally agreed to this interview, having turned others down over the years.

"He was shot," Charlie said. "During a raid."

He swallowed hard, his hands trembling visibly now despite their tight grip on his knees. The sun had shifted, casting long shadows across the lawn, but he seemed unaware of the changing light.

"He asked me," Charlie continued, his voice growing hoarse, "if he was going to see his mum again." He closed his eyes briefly. "What do you say to that? What words can possibly…"

He left the sentence unfinished. The wind moved through the garden, stirring the roses. The interviewer shifted slightly in his seat, clearly aware that they had ventured into deeper emotional waters than perhaps either of them had anticipated. He glanced briefly at his notes, then looked up with careful consideration.

"Did you ever feel anger?" he asked softly. "Towards the generals, the politicians – the people who sent you there?"

Charlie let out a sound that might have been a laugh in another lifetime, but now held bitterness. "Oh yes," he said, running a hand along the arm of his chair. "I felt a lot of things. Anger, certainly. Betrayal. Confusion. But mostly, as the years went by, just a deep, hollow sort of sadness."

The interviewer nodded, empathy evident on his face as he patiently gave Charlie time to speak.

Charlie rubbed his fingers together absently, as if trying to wash away stains that had long since faded. "They gave us medals, marched us through the streets when we finally came home – those of us who did come home. But no amount of medals or parades could bring back the lads who didn't make it. George Wray who used to sing hymns in the trenches when the shelling got bad. Or Robert Phillips, who carried a picture of his newborn daughter. Or any of the others."

The interviewer nodded thoughtfully, genuine emotion showing through his professional demeanour. "And what about those who did make it home? Did you feel… relief?"

Charlie's hands stilled in his lap as he considered the question. Relief? No, that wasn't the right word at all. Relief suggested an ending, a conclusion, a weight lifted. What he had felt – what he still felt – was something far more complex.

"There's a peculiar thing that happens when you survive something like that," he said, choosing his words carefully. "You look at all the names on the memorial in the town square, and you wonder…" He stopped, his jaw working silently for a moment. "Why? Why did I make it home when so many others didn't?"

The interviewer was quiet for a moment, allowing the impact of Charlie's words to linger. Then, cautiously, he asked, "Did you ever find an answer to that question?"

Charlie's lips pressed into a thin line, the corners turning down slightly. "No," he admitted finally. "And I doubt I ever will. The randomness of it all – that's what gets you in the end. Why did that shell land there and not here? Why did that bullet find him and not me? There's no rhyme or reason to any of it. Just blind luck."

The interviewer glanced at his notes again, then met Charlie's gaze with quiet curiosity.

"What was it like," he asked, "when you finally came home?"

Charlie exhaled slowly, settling back in his chair. A passing cloud momentarily dimmed the sunlight, and he watched its shadow race across the manicured lawn.

"Strange," he said after a long moment. "Like walking into someone else's life. I'd dreamed of home for four years – the smell of my mother's baking, the feeling of a proper bed. But when I got there, I..." He shook his head, searching for words to describe that peculiar displacement. "I felt like a stranger in my own life. Everything was exactly as I remembered it, but I wasn't the same person who had left."

"Was it difficult, adjusting to civilian life?"

Charlie huffed a short laugh, though there was no humour in it. "That's putting it mildly." He paused, considering. "You know, they never told us about that part. They trained us how to fight, how to kill. But nobody ever taught us how to come back."

He looked past the interviewer, his gaze distant.

"I remember my first night home," he continued. "December 1918. The house was so quiet it felt like my ears were ringing. No shells, no guns, no screaming. Just silence. I was lying in my old bed for hours, staring at the ceiling, waiting for something that wasn't coming."

The interviewer spoke carefully, his voice gentle. "Did things get easier? With time?"

Charlie considered the question, watching a pair of sparrows squabble over something in the flower bed. The world had changed so much since 1918, yet here he sat, still carrying the weight of those four years at war as if they had happened yesterday.

"Yes," he said eventually. "But not quickly. And never completely. The dreams still come. Less often now, but they still come. And certain sounds – backfiring cars, fireworks on Guy Fawkes Night – they can still take you right back there, just for a moment."

The interviewer flipped to the final page of his notes. The cameraman signalled quietly that they were running low on film, but no one seemed eager to rush this moment.

His gaze steady but respectful, the interviewer looked up. "Do you think it was worth it?" he asked Charlie. "All the pain, the loss... the years that followed. Was it worth it?"

Charlie exhaled slowly through his nose, a long, measured breath. The question wasn't unexpected – he'd asked it himself often enough over the years, lying awake in the small hours of the morning when the memories were closest to the surface.

He looked out across the garden, watching as the sun painted the flowers in shades of gold and amber. The trees stood tall and quiet, their branches swaying gently in the breeze, untouched by war, untouched by time. The world had healed its visible wounds, even if the invisible ones remained.

Finally, he turned back to the interviewer.

"No," he said firmly.

The word hung in the air between them, simple but heavy with meaning.

The interviewer didn't seem surprised by the

answer. He didn't speak immediately, allowing the moment its proper weight. The camera continued to roll, capturing the subtle play of emotions across Charlie's face.

Charlie's voice was calm but carried an underlying steel as he continued. "We thought we were fighting for a better world," he said. "But what we really did was send an entire generation of men into the ground."

His hands tightened slightly on the arms of his chair, his knuckles whitening briefly before relaxing again.

"I don't regret doing what I thought was my duty," he said, "but I regret that any of us had to do it at all. We thought we were fighting the war to end all wars. But look at what's happening now. There was Korea, and now there's Vietnam, all these new conflicts sprouting up like weeds. It seems we didn't learn much at all."

The interviewer swallowed, nodding. "That's... that's a powerful statement."

Charlie didn't waver. "It's the truth. And that's why I agreed to this interview, you know.

Because maybe if enough of us tell the truth about what war really is, what it does to men's souls, maybe the next generation will think twice."

A long silence stretched between them, filled only by the soft whir of the camera and the gentle rustle of leaves in the breeze.

The interviewer eventually cleared his throat, offering a small, respectful smile. "Thank you for sharing your story with us, Mr Greenly."

Charlie nodded once, decisively. "You're welcome. It needed to be said."

"Cut," called the director, and the camera stopped rolling.

The garden settled into a different kind of quiet as the crew began packing up their equipment. Charlie remained seated, his mind still on the muddy fields of France, on the faces of friends long gone. The war had ended fifty-five years ago, but it lived on in the memories of men like him, in the faded photographs on mantelpieces across Britain, in the stone monuments that stood in every village and town.

And now, at least, one more voice had been preserved. One more story saved from the relentless march of time.

As the shadows lengthened across the lawn and the evening air grew cool, Charlie finally stood, accepting with quiet dignity the help of a young production assistant. He walked slowly back towards the garden gates, his steps measured but steady.

Behind him, the garden lay peaceful in the fading light, the roses nodding gently in the breeze, the birds returning to their evening songs. The world had moved on, as it always did.

Chapter Eleven

The house was quiet, but not uncomfortably so. In the peaceful hush of a winter's evening in 1974, a fire burned low in the hearth, its amber flames casting dancing shadows across the wallpaper Charlie's wife had chosen thirty years ago. The soft glow illuminated the collection of photographs arranged on the carved oak mantelpiece – a timeline of precious memories captured in silver gelatin and early colour film, each frame holding a piece of the life he'd built after returning from the war.

There was his wedding photo from 1920, taken outside this very house. Charlie stood straight in his newly-pressed uniform, his medals gleaming. He'd been reluctant to wear them, but Margaret had insisted, saying they were part of who he was, part of the path he had walked. She stood beside him in that photograph, radiant in her mother's reworked wedding dress, her dark hair swept up beneath a veil of lace. Even now, the sight of her young face in that moment made Charlie smile.

Next to it sat a photograph from 1925, showing their children playing in the back garden on a sun-drenched afternoon. Young Thomas pushed his little sister Louise on the rope swing Charlie had hung from the old oak tree. The camera had caught them mid-laugh, their faces bright with the kind of innocent joy that Charlie had feared might vanish from the world during those dark days in the trenches.

And there, in the newest frame, were his grandchildren, gathered around him at his seventy-fourth birthday celebration just last summer. The five of them, aged six to sixteen, had their arms wrapped around his shoulders as they posed for the photograph.

Charlie lay in the brass bed that had been his and Margaret's since their wedding day, his body worn thin by the passage of years. His breathing came steady but shallow now, each inhalation a little less certain than the last. The silver hair at his temples had long since spread across his whole head, and his hands had grown frail, marked by liver spots and prominent veins.

Yet the years, for all their challenges, had been kinder than he'd dared to hope when he'd returned from France. The survivor's guilt that had threatened to consume him had slowly transformed into a determination to live well, to honour those who never had the chance to grow old.

His marriage to Margaret was wonderful. They had met at a church social in the spring of 1919, introduced by a mutual friend who had insisted that a war hero ought to have someone to dance with. Together, they had raised three children – Thomas, Louise, and William – watching with quiet pride as they grew into adults who understood both the value of peace and the price of freedom. He had worked as a clerk for the railway, a steady job that provided for his family and kept him busy.

His grandchildren had brought a joy he hadn't known his heart could still hold. He had taught them to fish in the stream where he and James had spent countless summer days before the war. He had told them stories – not of the trenches or the gas attacks or the friends he'd lost, but of courage in all its forms, of kindness in the face of darkness, of the importance of remembering history while still embracing life.

Now, in the quiet of his familiar bedroom, with the night pressing soft and dark against the windowpanes, Charlie knew with the same certainty that his own story was drawing to a close. His breaths came more slowly now, each one a little shallower than the last. The familiar aches in his joints seemed to be receding, as if his body was gradually releasing its hold on physical sensation.

Though his eyes were growing heavy, he was acutely aware that he was not alone in what he suspected might be his final hours. The house creaked with familiar movements – the sound of his children moving about downstairs, their voices carrying up the narrow staircase in hushed tones. He could hear Thomas explaining something to his own children in the kitchen, Louise's gentle shushing, and William's heavy tread on the bottom step.

A warm hand slipped into his own – Margaret's touch, as familiar to him as his own heartbeat. Her grip remained sure and steady. She had been his anchor through every storm, every nightmare, every moment of doubt. She squeezed his hand gently, her wedding ring pressing against his fingers.

"I'm here, love," she murmured, her voice carrying the same warmth it had held when she'd accepted his fumbling proposal in 1919, when she'd soothed his night terrors in the earlier days of their time together.

Now he felt a peace he hadn't known in decades. Her presence, steady and unwavering, wrapped around him like a soft blanket, chasing away the cold. He turned his head just slightly, enough to glimpse her face, softened by age but still so unmistakably Margaret. His lips twitched, a weak smile breaking through the haze of exhaustion.

Her voice came again, soft as a prayer. "It's alright, Charlie. Rest now, my love."

He let his eyes close, allowing himself to drift into the gathering darkness. The sound of his wife's breathing beside him, the distant murmur of his children's voices, and the gentle crackling of the fire all blended into a soothing lullaby.

Charlie dreamed, but not of war.

Gone were the familiar nightmares of shell bursts and poison gas, of rats scurrying through trenches and the endless, sucking mud. Instead, his mind carried him back to the summer of 1914, before the world changed forever. He was running through the meadow by the river, the grass high around his legs, the air heavy with the scent of wild lavender and clover. In the distance, he could hear his mother's voice calling him home for supper, the same way she had every evening of his childhood. He felt his father's strong hand on his shoulder, offering silent approval.

And there was James, whole and unchanged, the summer light catching his hair as he stood several feet away in the grass, as if the war had never happened. His familiar grin spread across his face, the same expression he'd worn when they'd walked into the recruitment office together, before they understood what warfare truly meant.

"Come on, Charlie," James called, his voice carrying across the years without effort. "We're going home."

Charlie smiled, feeling lighter than he had in sixty years. The step he took forward was effortless, unburdened by old wounds and arthritis. The weight of memory, of survival, of years of carrying the dead with him – it all fell away like autumn leaves in a gentle breeze.

For the first time since that summer day when he'd lied about his age to the recruitment officer, claiming eighteen when he was barely fifteen, Charlie was just a boy again. The world was full of possibility, unmarked by the scars of war and unimaginable loss.

****

Margaret did not immediately cry. Though grief was already beginning to well up inside her, she sat quietly, holding Charlie's hand, committing to memory the peaceful expression on his face.

Beneath the grief, there was a profound sense of gratitude. Charlie had survived when so many others hadn't. He had come home from France, had built a life and a family, had created a legacy of love and resilience that would live on through their children and grandchildren.

Now, at last, he was at peace. The memories that had haunted him for so long could no longer reach him. The pain he'd carried in his body and soul had finally released its hold.

Margaret lifted his hand to her lips, pressing a gentle kiss to his knuckles. "Sleep well, my love," she whispered, her voice steady despite the tears that had begun to fall. "Sleep well."

***

The funeral was held a week later, a small and dignified affair. Despite the winter chill, many came to pay their respects. Charlie's wife, children and grandchildren stood together near the grave, their hands clasped in shared grief and support.

As the service concluded, Margaret stepped forward to place one last poppy on the polished wood of the coffin. Her fingers lingered for a moment on its smooth surface, a final farewell to the man who had been the centre of her world for more than five decades.

Then, as the winter wind stirred the bare branches of the churchyard yews, she stepped back, straightened her shoulders, and let him go.

The world had changed beyond recognition since that summer of 1914, when young boys had marched away to war believing they'd be home by Christmas. The trenches where Charlie had fought had since given way to peaceful farmland, the remnants of war gradually softened by time and nature.

But Charlie's story, like the stories of all who had lived through those momentous times, would endure. It would live on in the memories of his family, passed down through his grandchildren, who would tell their own children about their grandfather. They would remember not just the soldier, but the man – the way he laughed, the way he worked, the way his eyes sometimes drifted to places no one else could see.

A soldier. A survivor. A husband, father, and grandfather.

A man who bore the memories of the fallen and honoured them in the gentle persistence of a life well lived.